T0354991

D MINOR

STORIES

LAURA OTIS

D MINOR
STORIES

iUniverse books may be ordered through booksellers or by contacting:

iUniverse
1663 Liberty Drive
Bloomington, IN 47403
www.iuniverse.com
844-349-9409

Because of the dynamic nature of the Internet, any web addresses or links contained in this book may have changed since publication and may no longer be valid. The views expressed in this work are solely those of the author and do not necessarily reflect the views of the publisher, and the publisher hereby disclaims any responsibility for them.

Any people depicted in stock imagery provided by Getty Images are models, and such images are being used for illustrative purposes only.
Certain stock imagery © Getty Images.

Author photo credit:
Joe Boris: © 2012 www.JoeBoris.com

ISBN: 978-1-6632-6347-6 (sc)
ISBN: 978-1-6632-6348-3 (e)

Library of Congress Control Number: 2024915363

Print information available on the last page.

iUniverse rev. date: 08/05/2024

CONTENTS

D MINOR

D minor sounds deep brown, brown that
    catches the soul in its current.
Brown like a varnished, fallen chestnut, rich
    swirls of chocolate darkness.
Coffee-brown like Beethoven's Ninth, so
    forceful it's nearly black.
Heart-flooding brown: Mozart's Requiem.
    Passion. Fear. The will to live.
"Ain't No Grave Can Hold My Body Down."
    Brown as the bass of Johnny Cash.
Brown like soft ridges of fresh-plowed earth,
    grooved tree bark, steaming dung.
Brown as the hide of an old buffalo, weary but
    ready to charge.
Brown whose force allows no rest as long as life
    can hear.

CONCERT OF WISHES

The neighbors' dryer was whining on a high D. On her Nordic ski machine, Megan stopped in midstride. She hadn't sung with a choir in months, but she knew the D, clean and bright, slicing the machine's whir like a shard of glass.

Didi had marveled that Megan could recognize notes and produce them on demand. She could name the key of a swirling organ piece by closing her eyes and listening. Music wandered, and Megan would breathe through its turns, following until it came home. She hummed the keynote, and then she knew: brown D minor; purple F major. Didi thought she was finding the notes from her A, which she could sing any place, any time. But Megan knew the notes as individuals. To find a D, you didn't reach down a fifth from an A. That would be like identifying a fig by holding it up against an orange.

Megan's sense for notes eluded most singers in the Linberg choir where she and Didi sang. During breaks, he hovered close. It piqued him that she could sit surrounded by people, staring at an overhead spot as if it held a node to another universe. To break her gaze, he waved a lean arm, the most restless part of his whiplash body.

"What are you seeing?" he asked, his blue eyes searching the air.

Late one night, after rehearsal, he hugged her until her ribs cracked, and she cried out with fear.

"I want you," he whispered in her ear.

Slowly, he eased his grip.

Didi invited her on bicycle tours, and together they rushed through shaded woods. They glided through wet spring forests, listening for cuckoos' calls. Didi imitated the birds so well he could enthrall one for minutes as it tried to impress the human impostor. Cuckoos sang a descending minor third—a sad, playful interval. Sometimes a confused bird sang a major third, an interval Didi loved. He called Megan *Terz*, his major third, pure and clean if sung just right, maddening when missed.

One morning, in a beech forest, their eyes met in wonder, and they braked together.

"*Ein Quart-Kuckuck*!" breathed Didi.

High in the pale green leaves, a cuckoo had sung a descending fourth, "Here Comes the Bride" in reverse. Didi sang the fourth back to the bird, but the cuckoo wouldn't answer.

Didi had a wife, a generous creature who tended plants in the Botanical Garden. He also had a girlfriend, a fierce, dark woman who worked in an art museum. In Megan's fifty-nine years of life, people had wanted her for their own agendas. She had left her husband years ago, when he'd said he longed to see her dead. No one craved her soul as Didi did, and she resolved to fight. She didn't want to be a wife, an owned object. The thought that *my wife* could sum up her whole being made her stomach clench. She thought she might displace the girlfriend, as though challenging for second-seat cello. Didi had spent years with smoky Gisela, who sang tenor in the choir.

LAURA OTIS

He came to Megan in the early mornings, when she was still warm with sleep. His skin felt moist and cool, bathed by the air on his ride to work. He slid into bed beside her, and their bodies quickly joined. His clear eyes widened, and drops of his sweat splashed her forehead. She held him as she watched the clock's blue digits, just breathing, just being. Didi dressed quickly and left a gift on her counter: a white bag of soft, buttered pretzels.

One day, after a rain shower, they rode side by side, holding hands as they whizzed past lush garden plots. Didi sat erect in a yellow sweater, at ease without touching his handlebars.

"We must never forget this time," he said to her with a deep smile.

Megan thought it was strange. Their souls had joined, yet he talked as though their time would end.

Didi wanted to stop after the first summer, when she flew back to Aliketa to teach. It exhausted him to serve three women, all of whom expected what Megan was getting. The logistics took genius, and the emotions frayed him. Megan considered the judgment of Solomon. If she loved him, shouldn't she resign her share? But she rebelled against the looming sacrifice. Why did the laws of virtue always demand that a woman stifle herself?

On the phone that fall, Didi maintained his presence. On his lunch break, he called from Linberg, demanding to hear her A. Three thousand miles away, she sang the bright tone, which he tested on a keyboard.

4

"Bingo!" he said.

Sometimes she failed.

"That was almost a G," he reproached.

Megan's A sharpened when she was excited and sank when she felt gloom. Ravaged by reading and grading, she couldn't meet Didi's demands. She had to maintain her bicycle. She had to buy only organic food. With secret delight, she bought a plastic box crammed with illicit strawberries.

When she returned to Linberg the next summer, Didi's impatience mounted. Megan was slow in everything she did. She was clumsy; she was socially awkward. She noticed nothing around her. Fogged in by her thoughts, she could have overlooked a pink gorilla. Didi said he wanted to be an older brother to guide her. He shouted when she broke a traffic rule she didn't know existed. He radiated disgust, and when he came inside her, he seemed disgusted with himself. He didn't leave her until a year later, the day she arrived to spend a year in Germany.

During that fellowship year, Megan cried all day every day. Her tears began when she became conscious. She cried while making breakfast in the kitchen where Didi had left white bakery bags. She cried while biking to work in the rain, cold wetness blending with her hot grief. Her tears paused when she entered the research institute where she worked and resumed the moment she left. She cried at the supermarket, the gym, and as she wandered through the gaping streets. She rode her bicycle through late-night blackness and lost herself among warehouses, unable to find a bridge over the dark river. She cried naked on her kitchen floor as a raw alto sang on the radio. The cold stone soothed her skin, and she welcomed its hardness. She beat her thighs with her fists and found satisfaction in the thuds. She slapped her face, then made rakes of her fingers and gouged red furrows into her skin.

With her fingertips, she found the slow pulse where the blood rose toward her brain. She brought her sharpest serrated knife to the spot where the skin was throbbing. Day after day, she watched herself in the mirror, her face swollen and monstrous, the silver biting her throat. She stripped naked and lay in her white tub so that when her blood ran out, she wouldn't leave a mess. She pressed hard and willed herself to cut—one, two, *three*—but the knife wouldn't budge. She wanted a different death, a death with a billion witnesses. She wanted to spray Didi with her brains and blood. Or no—she'd rather be stained with his blood. She wanted to see his flesh fly.

Didi called her each day, and sometimes he met her, once on a park bench beside a dry creek. Her endless tears aroused his rage.

"If you tell my wife, I'll do something really bad to you," he said. "It's not in my nature, but something will occur to me."

Megan's insides turned cold.

"*Wirklich fies*," he said. Something mean, nasty, and low. Probably he would use his technological skills to end her days as a professor.

She didn't want to tell his wife, whose eyes glowed green when she felt joy. Didi's lack of trust shook Megan—his belief she must be threatened into silence. He had been coming inside her body for two years, and she meant nothing to him.

"Das Leben ist kein Wunschkonzert," he told her. Life is no concert of wishes, a concert where they take requests.

Megan told her friends she wanted to end her life, and they urged her to come home. But that was what Didi sought: for Megan to disappear. Should she give up her fellowship, quit the choir, and withdraw to Aliketa, a conquered thing? Didi had suffered no consequences and was happy to be rid of her. His wife had never sensed the river softening the ground under her feet. Gisela seemed to have suspected but now walked secure in her triumph. After rehearsals, she and Didi rode off together; their taillights formed twin red stars in the night. Megan's joining with Didi hadn't meant enough to leave memories. An Alzheimer's relationship, she thought: last in, first out.

Grimly, perversely, Megan persisted. Didi would have to see her. She sang every rehearsal, church service, and concert. She finished her fellowship and flew home to teach. She wrote essays, blog posts, stories, and novels; she graded papers by the hundred. She earned a new degree and published a book on how "Let go, and move on" served abusers and bullies. Any time she wasn't needed in a classroom, she flew to Linberg, not just summers and holidays but spring and fall breaks.

In high school, she had clashed with a sharp-chinned girl who said people should eliminate desire. Megan had argued that desire was life, and without it, no life remained. But once her tears for Didi vanished, so did any twinge of lust. Grudgingly, she acknowledged that the girl might have been right.

Losing desire for a man was like waking from a nightmare into a world of overlooked pleasures. She delighted in the lint roller that left her fleece jacket black and the horn that eased her feet into stiff shoes. She felt as much need to be filled by a man as to be stabbed by a knife. When she saw Didi after a grueling semester, a hearing aid was peeping from one ear. She wondered what had drawn her to this gray, faded man, who still seemed to wish she'd disappear.

The pandemic must have been a godsend to Didi, since Megan was banned from Germany. The US president scorned the virus, which afflicted only the weak. Anyone strong had nothing to fear—as he showed when it breached his frame. The Germans pointed to the nine million cases, the 230,000 Americans dead. Megan's waxy blue passport meant no more than a shim to prop a leaning bookcase.

She found herself trapped in Aliketa, where, in late October, pink camellias dropped petals on nodding goldenrod. She had treated the place as a gulag, a camp where she hunkered down to work. She had flown to Aliketa the night before classes started and soared off the evening they ended. During the semester, she'd left her apartment only to bike to campus or buy groceries at YourFood.

Aliketa's audacious life frightened her, defying human control. Date-sized roaches called palmetto bugs brazenly surveyed her kitchen counters. When she raised her eyes from her students' work, she peered into a jungle of crepe myrtles. Brilliant cardinals paused inches from her window, and orange wasps tapped the glass with dry heads. Squirrels gouged black dirt from her planters until her pink chrysanthemums starved on lonely islands of turf. Down the street, kudzu spilled cascades of green hearts into vacant lots. Volcanic heaves of roots broke the sidewalks into mad mosaics. Treacherous potholes marred the roads, deadly when she rode home at night. Water mains burst, leaving her taps dry. Pounding storms felled trees, which broke power lines strung like fiesta lights.

Just last week, she had clambered over a fallen oak blocking the fastest route to YourFood. The vine-covered trunk had risen almost to her waist, but an old man on the far side had hoisted her bike, and she had scrambled over. Didi would have been proud of her.

"*Ich bin stolz auf dich,*" she could hear his reedy voice say.

Early on, he had convinced her to sell her car, and her world had shrunk to a two-mile radius from her condo.

For the first time since Megan had moved to Aliketa, she watched spring grow into summer. She turned in her grades, and life found the rhythm for which she'd been born. She rose at five and walked at dawn to hear the birds' interwoven songs. High in the oaks, cardinals called, "Wick-wick-wick!" Towhees hopped in the bushes and cried, "Tree!"

9

Hummingbirds hovered before orange trumpet flowers, and black-and-white woodpeckers tapped scaly trunks. Soft pink azaleas dropped their petals and were replaced by blue hydrangea balls. As the heat intensified, fuchsia sprays of crepe myrtle dangled against the brilliant sky. Megan's legs burned as she climbed steep hills. When she came to a dead end, she paused, breathing hard, to contemplate grooved bark and wet leaves. In her peach-colored bedroom, she read all day: *Cyrano de Bergerac*, *In Search of Lost Time*. In the evening, she mounted her Nordic ski machine and kept it rasping for half an hour.

Cut off from Germany, though, she deteriorated. Her unbleached roots grew down to her ears, a gray-brown cap of dullness. Her hairs stuck together at the ends and gladly left her head when she tried to part them. The lining of her indigo jacket split apart into white shreds. Quarter-sized holes broke the rubber soles of her red boiled-wool booties. Where the balls of her feet met the road, her sneakers were ground to smooth planes. She could maintain nothing, replace nothing. If her laptop broke, she would be Helen Keller in her no-world, an unknown soul drifting in blackness.

To dull her fear, Megan found a pleasure that Germany couldn't offer. In Linberg, she could watch ten TV channels tops; in Aliketa, she had over a thousand. While she ate, exercised, and cleaned her space, she sampled other worlds. Bickering couples turned moldy homes into gray beauties on emerald squares. The home renovators inspired her—the blast of sledgehammers, the glint of bright tile. She wished those couples could annihilate rot and save each dying house in the world. It struck her as criminal that people left houses to rats, termites, and squatters. But renovated and staged, all the homes looked alike: whitewashed caves with hints of orange and aqua.

Megan turned from the restorers to the police. Followed by cameras, cops rushed through neighborhoods Megan would never have dared enter. They smashed through doors and stormed into homes. Their rough panting chopped the air as they chased suspects they tackled or tased. Best of all, Megan loved the K9 units, whose German shepherds found fools cowering in black brush.

"Sheriff's office, ca-*nine*!" sang the pursuers. "Make yourself known, or you're gonna get bit!"

Megan pictured a lusty German shepherd closing her teeth on Didi's leg.

In late May, a sadistic cop killed a Black man by kneeling on his neck. Megan woke from a nightmare in which a heavy leg was crushing her own throat. Despite the pandemic, people spilled into the streets, and she joined the marching crowds. Awkwardly, she wheeled her bike while holding a green sign that said, "Injustice to One Is Injustice to All."

Overnight, cop shows disappeared from the air. In a nation with 2.3 million in prison, favoring the cops' viewpoint didn't seem fair. Still, Megan would have given her eyeteeth to watch one barking police dog tauten his leash. She scanned the channels for a police show that had escaped the purge, and she found *Murder*.

Murder shadowed big-city detectives trying to solve actual crimes. They tackled and tased no one—from the looks of them, that wouldn't have gone too well. Almost all the detectives were fat. The hot cops worked for the gang units. These big-bellied nerds tracked criminals on computers. They worked for thirty-six hours straight in cubicles, living on sour coffee and hardened pizza. In pairs, they interviewed miserable suspects, one poking while the other watched. They searched Facebook and traced phone records, but mostly, they drove.

With camera crews riding in their backseats, they rolled through desolate neighborhoods. The cameras studied signs of life—a burst of black birds rising from a bare tree, sneakers dangling from an electric wire. The detectives raised yellow police tape and shone flashlights on smears of blood. They knocked on rows of battered brown doors, asking, "You see anything unusual last night?" All day, all night long, the detectives kept searching.

Megan liked the Wichita crew best—above all, Detective Martin Blount. He moved with a grim, rolling walk. His small head with protruding ears seemed to have landed on the wrong bulky body. Stuffed into a bulletproof vest, he looked like an angry turtle. Blount kept what remained of his brown hair so short he might as well have had none at all. Round-shouldered and full-lipped, he scowled as he typed into his computer. When the camera hung close, Megan could feel his keystrokes match the rhythm of his breaths. His thick, square glasses with black rims shot gleams that hid his pale eyes. As he considered what his screen was telling him, he pursed his lips in a prissy way. In five months of watching *Murder*, Megan had never seen him smile. Blount was a homely wreck of a man, just a shade shy of ugly.

But Blount often spoke for his team. The straighter, more colorful cops nudged him forward. With clear eyes not quite blue, gray, or green, he looked straight into the camera. His voice came flat and tight, a spatula that cut dully.

"We can't bring these people back," he said. "But we can get justice for their families. We can give them that."

Whether or not a case was his, Blount steered into it, guiding his colleagues. Megan noticed that crimes against women outraged him most, especially if they turned up in dumpsters. More than once, the show started with a shin and ankle protruding from under a white pizza box. When a homeless woman was raped, strangled, and dumped, Blount reacted as though someone had rammed a cock into his own body. A close-up revealed the red pores of his nose and the hairs of his gray-blond eyebrows. His lips quivered.

"This is some sick rapist bastard," he said. "We've got to get this guy. He's got to pay for what he did."

Blount seemed to welcome the camera, and the camera loved him for it. His handsome colleagues stiffened before the lens; Blount spoke to the viewer on the far side. He talked of the city's poorest people and of the victims' families' pain. Artistic shots that began as blurs sharpened to close-ups of his blond lashes and gleaming rims. The blue of a shirt his wife must have bought turned his eyes to morning glories.

As he typed, the camera tracked the strokes of his fingers, one of them fused with a thick gold ring.

Some episodes featured the lead detectives and showed pictures of their families. The policemen's recklessness shocked Megan. Someday their suspects would be released from jail, and sometimes they didn't go at all. Stalkers, pedophiles—all kinds of hungry people were watching. Didn't the detectives fear being hunted? Blount proved to be one of the boldest, posting a picture of all four children. On her Nordic ski machine, Megan glimpsed his family in the downward stroke of one arm. She couldn't tell the wife from the oldest girl, but she made out five people and two dogs. Blount must have been blond in his youth, since his family matched their retrievers' fairness. They looked as though a bomb had gone off at the blond factory.

As Megan flailed on her ski machine that night, she kept her eyes on the television. Blount and his partner, Braverman, were questioning a suspect.

"Be honest with us. Tell us the truth," said Braverman, a twitchy, black-haired ex-marine.

"I am being honest with you, sir," answered a voice blurred to a dark smear.

Blount brought his index finger to his lips. As he considered the man's story, he pressed them softly, his fingertip lodged under his large nose.

Megan fingered a scratch on her arm, where the skin had broken in a loose ruffle. She smelled detergent, a cloying fog rising from her neighbors' dryer. Ever since new people had moved in downstairs, their dryer fumes had been polluting her space. Hot, linty mist surged up through their interconnected vents. In minutes, fog would fill her dryer and spill out in sickening waves. In a practiced round, she dismounted, snapped off the air-conditioning, and slid open the windows with heavy scrapes. She set the ceiling fans whirling and stopped, breathing hard. What would the chemical sludge do to her lungs? She pulled on a bitter-smelling mask and walked slowly downstairs.

Six units shared the gray entryway, and their inhabitants all breathed the same air. Two young women came and went in blue scrubs. A construction worker's boots dropped cakes of dirt, which crumbled to dust on the stairs. Someone left each morning at six, shaking the building with the door's slam. For years, the unit under Megan's had sat empty except for visits from the owner's parents. The cheerful old couple made coffee whose sweetness invaded Megan's bedroom closet. The kind pair stayed only a few days, and they never used the dryer. These new people seemed addicted to that whistling generator of hot air.

Megan rapped three times on their red door and wished she'd hit it harder. They might not hear her over the dryer's whine. The floor trembled as heavy steps approached. A man in a bright yellow T-shirt opened the door and stared at her defensively. A helmet of thick white hair stuck close to his head. His egg-like belly stretched his canary shirt far out from his beige shorts.

"Yes?" he asked in a broad voice.

"Hi." Megan hoped her smile looked real. "I'm Megan. I live upstairs. I—I just wanted you to know that when you run your dryer, it empties into my apartment—the exhaust. I think it happens with a lot of these units. I'm hoping we can find a way to fix it."

The man frowned and folded his arms so that his muscles flexed. "I'll talk to Jenna about it," he said. "We're cousins of hers. Just staying here for a while."

"Oh yeah!" Megan's face felt warm. "I know her parents. Nice people. They stay here sometimes too."

The white-haired man exhaled, and his shoulders dropped a few degrees. "Well, I'll talk to her," he said. "See if anyone's complained about this before."

A shadow flickered on the bare white wall behind him.

"I'd appreciate it," said Megan. "That detergent smell fills my apartment. I have to open all the windows."

"Are you allergic?" called an alto voice.

Against the white wall appeared a woman who must have been drinking in each word. She looked taller than her husband, maybe because of her stand-up brown hairdo. She gazed at Megan while she spoke, but she didn't approach the door.

"I don't think I'm allergic," said Megan, "but the scent makes it hard to breathe. Do you use dryer sheets?"

"Yes," answered the woman without moving. "I can stop using those. I can stop doing that immediately."

"Thank you," said Megan. "I'd really appreciate it."

"We'll talk to Jenna. See what she says."

"Thank you." Megan nodded.

The man swung the door shut.

Megan walked back up the scarred gray stairs, wondering who these people could be. They looked to be about her age—fifty-nine a few weeks ago. Why would a sixty-year-old couple with no kids run their dryer for hours each day? Maybe the man was incontinent, and his wife had to wash their soaked sheets. That would hit a man hard if he liked to be in charge. Maybe he had run a business, which he'd lost in the pandemic along with their house. They might have moved up from Florida, where he'd managed a restaurant or charter boat line. He or his wife might have found work in Aliketa, but they seldom left the space under her own. She suspected the woman, not the fat-bellied man, of falling in love with the dryer. Maybe the warm, humming thing reminded her of the vast house she'd lost and hoped to find again.

On the threshold of her space, Megan stood on one foot, scratching her itchy shin with one rubber heel. A dime-sized red welt had risen on her leg, probably from some mosquito who'd stuck her. In an uneven trio, Blount and Braverman continued to grill their suspect. As Megan walked toward their voices, she saw a black spot that broke the pattern on her tan-and-white couch. She had never studied its cappuccino stripes from this angle. Was that dark speck part of a tag? Close-up, the spot spread to a blur, so she pulled on her glasses. The dark fleck was a red-brown cylinder, like an iron-rich vitamin pill. Sticky white threads held the chestnut capsule against the couch. She pulled it loose and tossed the brazen, organic thing out the window.

Without pulling off her dirty sneakers, she walked into the bedroom. "Palmetto bug egg case," she typed into her laptop, and a grid of red-brown pills filled the screen.

She reached down to rub her itching shin and scratched the round bump until it burned. She would have to inspect her whole space. How many egg cases were there? Didi had warned her about these eggs when she'd described the scrabbling brown visitors to her kitchen.

"You must never squash a roach," he'd said, "because in dying, they eject an egg case that will hatch a thousand."

Apparently, they also squeezed out egg cases when they were hale with life. Megan raised the couch's cushions and found two more dark pills lying like lost licorice pieces. Another had landed beside the couch, birthed too quickly to be secured. She pulled the bulky couch from its place against the wall and tipped it over, breathing hard. Should she tear up her bed, haul the dishes from their cabinets, spill a thousand books from her bookcases? From below, the high D sang on like the whirling bit of a drill.

As Megan gathered roach egg cases, Blount and Braverman failed to break their suspect. He asked for a lawyer, and wearily, they pushed themselves up. They withdrew down their dim, carpeted hallway, and the camera followed their receding backs. Subtitles over their crusted coffeepot said the man hadn't been charged, and the investigation continued.

Megan scratched the bump on her leg and a red scrape across her arm. Her fingertips came back wet. The itchy lumps must have been oozing. She wiped her fingers on her thigh and reassembled her couch, piece by piece. She inspected each tan-and-white cushion before shoving it in place, but she found no more dark pills. No palmetto bugs would hatch there that night. She left everything else intact and withdrew to bed.

Megan woke up burning in blue darkness.

"I've never experienced anything like this," said a voice.

Blount's hard-edged tones had awakened her, but the round man had disappeared. From the unit below came her neighbor's snores—low, rasping bars of sound. Inside her, every cell felt like a furnace. Her breath lost its rhythm, and she gasped in panic. *The virus!*

Megan's heart galloped, and she snapped on the light. On her right forearm, sticky white peaks were erupting into a red mountain range. The dime-sized pink bump on her leg had grown to a half-dollar. Brown and yellow stains had marred her peach-ice-cream sheets. The clock said 3:23 a.m.; the thermometer, 98.8. For Megan, that might have meant a fever, since she rarely broke 97.

She padded into the kitchen for water, shielding her eyes from the flood of light. On the sink's silver rim, a thumb-sized brown creature froze, a dark bar hanging from her backside. Megan slapped at her with a blue rubber glove, which smacked the shining steel sink. The roach rocketed across the white dish drainer like a pitted date on legs. Megan ran for the broom, since the bug was racing down the cabinet toward the floor. The roach flattened herself into a corner, where Megan's clumsy swipes failed to dislodge her. Didi had been right. She was too slow, but this birth-giving thing outraged her.

Megan pulled aside chairs silent on felt pads Didi had made her apply. She grasped the broom's blue bar and stabbed at the brown invader. Guilt seized her for a moment: she was attacking a life-giving female. The blue nylon bristles tore the bug loose and shot her across the floor. The roach righted herself and streaked for the hall door. Megan followed and seized the knob. One last swipe left the bug in the hallway, spinning under the brilliant light. Megan closed the door and locked it. No espresso pill lay on the floor. The brave bug had held on to her egg case, and as soon as Megan went to bed, she might crawl back in to give birth beside the silver lake or the tan-and-white mountains she loved.

Megan scratched her oozing arm through her nightgown so that her nails wouldn't draw blood. The white flannel yellowed and stuck to her skin, so she covered the welts with Band-Aids. The white gauze centers wouldn't cover the wounds, which suffocated under pink plastic. The diagonal red gash across her arm looked like a failed attempt to amputate her hand. Once the wet bumps were covered, she could scratch again, which she had to do each thirty seconds. The itch jeered at her, and she groaned as her nails flattened it to a burn.

Megan didn't have COVID, but she had something else. The poison must have come from that fallen tree. As she'd clambered over the trunk, her palm had met a network of vines. She'd spotted dark ivy leaves but none of the heart-shaped triads she had feared all her life. When she had climbed trees as a girl, poison ivy had swelled her face like a pumpkin and puffed her eyes shut. Her mother, who'd seen Megan's ailments as time theft, had stiffened with disgust. Back then, the bumps hadn't oozed yellow juice. Something else must have entered through the gashes. She would have to talk to a doctor—right after she taught her 8:00 and 11:00 classes.

The next morning, Megan armed herself with tissues, which shrank and yellowed as she mopped. Her students signed in loyally, some from China, some wrapped in blankets, some with their home squares black. As she talked about metaphors, she wiped her arm. A urine-colored drop hit the space bar.

After class, when a steer-necked doctor appeared on her screen, her voice broke as she thanked him for seeing her.

"What have you got for me?" he asked in tones that echoed Braverman's.

Megan set her laptop on the floor and eased her shin toward the camera until her welts filled her square.

"Oh yeah," he muttered.

He prescribed cortisone and antibiotics, and the fight began. The red rash had overrun much of Megan's right arm and leg. She smeared on gobs of cream and covered them with white pads held by sticky tape. She washed her filthy nightgown and sheets, which soon became spotted with grease. The itching lessened, but sometimes she gouged between the pads and groaned. On Zoom, she told her students of her ailment, since they must have wondered why she was scratching. The dryer sang, and she opened the windows. Tiny black bugs explored the walls, and she watched indifferently.

Now she had Blount to comfort her. He had never felt anything like what she made him feel. When she awoke at 3:30 a. m., she ground circles into her mattress, imagining his awe at his own desire. She fell asleep nestled against his belly, one of his thin arms draped over her side. When she washed her face, she rammed the sink with tireless hips.

Despite his exhausted looks, Martin Blount might well be younger than she. His hair had left him long ago, and his belly flowed freely. Obsidian curves darkened the skin under his eyes, but jobs that forbade sleep aged you fast. Blount might be under fifty, maybe even in his midforties.

Neither he nor anyone else wanted the lust of a fifty-nine-year-old woman. Megan knew almost no one in her fifties. Fifty-year-olds stood deep in the human pyramid, with sneakered feet crushing their shoulders. They worked endlessly, out of sight, fulfilling twenty- and eighty-year-olds' needs. A fifty-nine-year-old woman craving a younger man would meet the same amused disgust as a dog trying to mate with a man's leg. First, he would shake it off with laughter, then hurl it loose with repulsion. If Blount knew she cried his name in the dark, he would look at her as he looked at his suspects: with the incredulity of an outraged father staring down an amoral teenager.

But 3:30 a.m. had its own logic. Martin Blount would want her, and he would come.

She had witnessed a murder. More than witnessed—a drive-by shooter had killed her brother, spraying her with his blood. Blount had driven her straight downtown, and he sat facing her across a gleaming fake-wood table. As he leaned forward, his gray eyes sought hers and then quickly broke their gaze. Megan rubbed a stiff patch in her hair that must have caught a splash of blood.

She knew nothing of the killers; all she had seen was a gun pointing from a car like an accusing finger. Her brother's secret vice had burst through into the life he was trying to shield. He must have owed someone money, or maybe he'd stolen someone's drugs.

As Blount wrote, he pressed his lips with his index finger. When he raised his eyes to Megan's, he seemed to read her—her crusted hair, her shaking fingers. She counted three breaths before he spoke.

"I'm going to give you my card," he said. "And the card of my partner, Jim Braverman. Call us if you think of anything. Do you have anyone? Is there someone you can go to right now?"

"I'll be all right," said Megan.

Blount kept his gray-blue eyes on her as she rose.

Three nights later, she was watching *Murder*, when a knock jolted her alert. Not a buzz but an actual knock—human bones against her wooden door. Megan's heart burst to life. She breathed from her belly and called in her strongest voice.

"Who is it?"

"Wichita PD. Detective Blount."

Blount was wearing a sky-blue shirt secured by a navy-blue tie. His black shoes gleamed in the warm light. His shirt and black pants fit him oddly, taut over the belly, loose in the shoulders and legs. Still, the colors suited him. He must have dressed up for a TV crew. His eyes scanned her room in a quick sweep and then settled on her.

"I came to check on you," he said. "See if you remembered anything. See if you were all right." His voice floated like a flat disk.

She smiled. "I didn't know you did that."

"We do."

Blount stepped toward her. Suddenly, she found herself pressed against him, as though caught by a wave on a calm shore. She dissolved into his warm, bittersweet smell. Through dark instants, she breathed with him. The rhythm quickened, and she squirmed to loosen his grip. Blount gazed at her with a look of awe.

"I saw you," he said, "and I felt something. I've never felt anything like it."

"I feel it too," she murmured. "But you don't have to do this. You can walk away now. You've done nothing wrong. Walk away."

Blount stroked her hair, and the force of his hand pulled her face upward. His eyes had borrowed some blue.

"No," he said. "I'm done walking away from everything beautiful and good."

He pulled off his glasses, which met her end table with a soft click.

Blount came to her almost every day. It shocked her how often he appeared, usually out of breath. Probably he parked blocks away, always in a different spot. He must have been lying not just to his wife but to his colleagues, who were harder to fool. Megan feared that in all those years of breaking liars, he hadn't learned how to hide the truth. Yet his grin when he saw her cast no shadows. He touched her as though he were born to do it.

Under the covers with Martin Blount, Megan felt alive as she hadn't in years. Blount said the same: he had married before he knew who he was, and he was breaking free from a chrysalis to flap his wings for the first time. He clutched her as though a wave might tear her from him, and he cried out when he came. Megan loved that she could make him arch his neck with pleasure. Most of all, she loved to watch him sleep—his lips parted, his fingers soft. In the blue light of her clock radio, his breath stirred the shadows in a slow rhythm. She had thought he would snore, but his breaths were sighs floating from every cell.

Sometimes she and Blount lay awake together, their voices blending in the dark.

"What's the hardest you've ever laughed?" she asked.

The darkness tightened as he thought and then relaxed as, suddenly, he knew.

"I was in Galveston," he said. "I come from down that way. Windy day, gigantic waves. Red flags all over the place. We weren't supposed to go in the water, but you know Texas. Gray sky, whipping wind—everyone out there. There were these three teenage guys—they'd bought a golden swan float. Huge. You and I could have ridden it to Cancún."

Megan stroked his hair, moist under her fingertips.

"Hey, quit that!" he said. "You're going to short-circuit my brain. I'm trying to tell you something here. So this giant swan float—beautiful thing, round hollow, curved neck. I saw it in a shop for fifty bucks. These guys had bought it to meet girls. They spot these three blonde girls in the surf, shivering in striped bikinis. 'Want to ride on the swan?' they ask, and the girls are game. But the waves keep spilling them over anytime they try to clamber on. This one girl—she was pretty sturdy, and she really wanted to mount that swan."

Megan jostled him, and he laughed.

"She'd throw one leg over it—thighs like turkey drumsticks—and almost get on, but then a wave would break and smash all six of them and me along with them, standing there watching. When I came up, they were all gasping, and the plastic swan was bobbing on the waves. Once, it almost got away, and the tallest guy went thrashing after it. I just started laughing. Happened over and over. 'Come on! You can do it!' *Boom!* None of them would quit. I kept getting knocked down and coming up laughing."

Megan squeezed him as he shook. She could see it—the golden swan, the determined girl, the eager guys.

"What about you?" he asked. "You tell me now. Funniest thing you ever saw."

Megan drew a breath, and she knew.

"There was this singing group," she said. "All women. Long time ago, when I was in school. I told them about this time I left a tampon in, and I forgot, and a doctor had to dig it out."

"You're kidding me," he said. "This is what women talk about when we're not there?"

"Yeah," she taunted. "Not about you. We're pretty much into our own parts."

Blount pinched her side, and she giggled.

"So, it turns out, this happens a lot. A whole bunch of the singers had forgotten things that squeamish doctors had to fish out. One woman acts out her gynecologist holding up a ripe tampon as if he were holding a dead mouse by the tail. We start laughing harder and harder, grabbing things around us that had been 'found.' Tissues. Candy wrappers. Gloves. The remote control. Then this woman, Elsie Dinkins, runs in from the living room with a floor lamp."

Blount clung to her as she laughed.

"That's alarming. Anything dangerous in there?" His voice reassembled itself. "I'd better investigate."

Still shaking, he clambered onto her and quickly slipped inside. She had come to love his sudden changes, and she gripped him with all her strength. His breathing harshened, and she saw the golden swan, loose and bobbing toward Cancún.

"Oh!" cried Blount.

And he lay still.

Megan called Braverman when the ambulance left. Until then, she had been numb. The dispatcher had made her press Blount's chest, and through dumb minutes, she had worked as a pump, following commands fed into her ear. Her hands slipped against Blount's wet skin, but when she blew air into him, his lips were dry. No movement stirred his fleshy features, even when she pinched his round nose. A paramedic with a ponytail took over, but she pumped him only a short while. Blount had died before she or Megan could save his heart.

Braverman rushed in, panting, every muscle of him tense. Blount's partner had always frightened Megan. He had brought along their boss, Sergeant Knight, the tallest and fattest of the crew. Even with his sparse gray hair, Knight stood so straight Megan felt as though she were facing two soldiers.

"You OK?" asked Knight. "Thanks for calling us."

Braverman started as his shoulder touched a picture frame. "He's at the hospital?" he demanded. "What was he doing here at 3:00 a.m.?" Braverman's black eyes challenged her.

"He—he came to check on me." Megan's voice trembled.

Knight was studying her from a different angle, and the men's gazes merged into a deadly beam.

"When they took him away, did he have any clothes on?" Knight asked softly.

Megan could barely shake her head.

"Fucking *cunt*!"

Braverman's hand struck her face, and she fell. She rolled toward the wall, but his taut legs followed.

"Fucking *bitch*! You know he has four kids? The little one's three."

Braverman's foot left a burning print of pain on her side. He brought his shaking hands to his face.

"Fucking hell! What are we gonna tell Lucy?"

Knight gripped his shoulder and pulled him back. The older man reached down to Megan and hauled her up. He pushed her toward the couch, where she landed roughly.

"He was talking to a witness." Knight's low voice rolled. "He was checking on a witness, and he just keeled over."

"Yeah, he was giving her his special brand of comfort."

Braverman's disgust singed her. His right hand twitched as though he were fighting an urge to hit her harder.

"Take it easy, Jimmy," said Knight. "Jeez! He made a choice. You know how he was about women."

Braverman shook his head and looked down with an incredulous smile.

Knight pointed a thick finger at Megan, who slowly drew herself up. She spread her fingers and pushed her palms into the dry, yielding couch.

"We're going to the hospital now," said Knight. "Someone will contact you for a statement. He came to check on you, and he collapsed. That's it. They took his clothes off when they treated him—or tried to. He didn't leave anything here, did he?"

Megan shook her head. The detectives' eyes scanned her cappuccino couch and, through an open door, her criminal bed. She would wash the sheets first thing tomorrow so that no trace of Blount remained.

"Other than that, I don't want to hear a peep out of you," said Knight. "You stay in this hole." His eyes circled the room. "Whatever this place is. If those four kids find out how their dad died—"

"We'll come to check on you." Braverman leered at her.

Knight drew a slow breath. He nudged Braverman toward the door, but then he turned.

"You've been through a lot," he said. "You may even have felt something for him. But you did wrong. You did wrong."

He shut the door so hard the floor trembled as Megan listened to their receding steps.

She tried to pause the images and rewind the way the detectives reversed their camera footage. She craved Blount's look of amazement before he kissed her, his astonishment at what life could bring. She wanted his flat voice, his cackle in the dark, surging inevitably toward her.

Lingering and dwelling worked well at night, but in the daytime, Braverman breached her thoughts. How dare she? These men were professionals, doing their job, and here she was, imagining them in bed like some geezer ogling stewardesses. At times, she felt the whole crew seize her limbs and hurl her from their space. Her horror fantasies didn't dull the urge to kiss Blount's pockmarked cheek.

Megan's students turned in eight-page drafts, every sentence of which needed pruning. In one weekend, she had to grade fifteen papers before essays from her other class arrived Monday. As she read, she gouged at the gap between the bandages under her legging. The itch no longer maddened her, but it irked. Each morning and night, she held her breath as she peeled away the white pads. They came off clean now, unmarked by ochre stains, but red horror still ruled her shin and forearm. Anyone who saw the lava on her skin might have retched.

"As an intelligent woman, it infuriates Maggie that she is not allowed to study," one paragraph began.

The high D of the dryer pricked Megan's ear. It had been whining since ten that morning, now eight hours ago. Each time it had whistled, she had opened the windows, through which frigid air crept. Outside, the steamy atmosphere had tightened, and vermillion leaves were dropping from crepe myrtle branches. Each time the fife stopped with a sudden glottal, hope moved her to shut the windows and turn on the heat. The last time the D had sounded, she had given up on closing the windows. Clutching her mouse with numb fingers, she hummed the D-minor flames of Mozart's Requiem.

Slowly, Megan pushed herself up from her chair. She

pulled on a blue N-95 mask and laced her black sneakers tightly. She didn't try to silence her steps, striking each stair with her whole foot. A wash of sound drifted from behind her neighbor's door, on which she thumped six times. The tomato-red door opened to reveal the white-haired man, who looked a little disheveled. His proud belly had shrunk, and his gray pants might have fallen if not held by a brown belt. His thick hair had contracted, its volume reduced by grease. Pork sizzled in a pan a few feet from where he stood.

"Hi," said Megan. "You guys doing all right?"

"Yeah, we're fine," he answered quickly.

A floorboard creaked to his right. The woman must have been tending the pork.

"I—I need to ask you about the dryer again," said Megan. "It's been going since ten this morning. I have to turn off the heat and open the windows when you use it, or I can't breathe. It's getting cold up there. We have to find a solution."

The man scowled and rerolled the sleeve of his blue shirt. "I talked to Jenna last time you came down," he said. "No one's ever had a problem with it before."

Megan swallowed. "I never had a problem—I'm the only one who's been up there—because the apartment was empty. No one was using the dryer."

The man folded his arms and fixed her with dark eyes. He blew out a long, slow breath. Megan stepped back toward the stairs.

"You want us to stop using our dryer?" he asked.

"Maybe—maybe you could use it less," said Megan. "In Germany, most people don't even have dryers. They use so much energy."

"No dryers?" The tall, brown-haired woman appeared behind his shoulder. Her drawn face looked incredulous.

"So why don't you go back there?" He raised an arm and pressed his palm against the doorframe.

"They won't let me in!" Megan's eyes were wet. "I can't go."

The weary man stayed framed in the doorway, blocking the light. Behind him, his wife studied Megan, as though waiting to see what she would do.

"Look, I'm sorry—but you can't come down here giving us orders," he said. "We've got a right to wash our clothes."

"For eight hours?" Megan's voice wavered. "What are you washing? I've got a right to breathe."

"You've got some nerve." The man's throat tightened as if he were holding words back. "Grinding away on that machine every night—right over our heads—when we're trying to eat. Feels like you're trying to scrape your way right through the ceiling."

"I—I'm sorry. Why didn't you say something? I could do it a different time."

Megan scratched her arm through her white cotton sleeve. Her wounds were itching as they hadn't in weeks.

"And that!" He pointed a thick finger at her bike as though trying to vaporize it. "You make this place look like a pigsty. This isn't some goddamn dorm."

Parked behind the stairs, her wheeled friend had shed black tears on the floor. On rainy days, the brake pads cried slate-gray mascara.

"You're not into cleaning, are you?" The man angled his chin toward his wife. "She cleans our place top to bottom each week. You run your washer once a week, if that. Since we moved here, you haven't run a vacuum cleaner once—not once! We've got palmetto bugs all over the place. There's a pandemic on!"

Tears soaked the rim of Megan's mask. "I don't bring the palmetto bugs," she said. "Vacuuming won't stop the pandemic."

The tall woman rubbed the heel of one hand over her head as though trying to flatten her hair. Thick and brown, the tufts stood like quills with not enough space to lie.

"Running around all day," he fumed. "God knows what you do up there. It's like having a goddamn squirrel in the attic."

"You want me to clean but not move?" asked Megan.

The man twitched as an impulse caught him, and she stepped back against the stairs. He drew a deep breath and folded his arms.

"Who's Martin?" he asked.

"George!" his wife gasped.

Megan shook as she inhaled.

"No, you tell me. I want to know." An ugly smile curved his lips. "Waking us up at four in the morning."

"You're not awake then! I can hear you snoring!" cried Megan.

"I'm not." His dark eyes shifted to his wife. "But she is."

"George, stop it!" Her thin face tightened with terror.

"No, I won't stop it!" George turned to face her. "All day long, you talk about her! She's calling for Martin; she doesn't clean. That machine of hers shreds your nerves. But you don't have the guts to tell her."

"He's sick!" Tears broke from his wife's reddened eyes. "I'm sorry. He doesn't know what he's saying."

"Don't tell her that!" he roared. "God damn it!"

He shoved her roughly, and she disappeared. Maybe she was scraping the pork, whose smell had darkened.

Megan tried to speak but could find no breath. The bristle-haired wife was telling stories about her. No doubt women who fell into holes fantasized about those in the world above. Megan rubbed her arm, although the itching had stopped.

"I'm going to talk to Jenna," said Megan. "I'm going to call the co-op board."

"Right," said the man disgustedly. "Call Martin."

He shut the door hard.

Megan's heart slammed blood through her as she walked upstairs and withdrew behind her red door. Whatever sickness George had, she hoped it would kill him as soon as possible.

Megan wanted so many people dead. First, this bully of a man. Then Didi, and her ex-husband. Shannon Murphy in junior high, who used to say, "You'd better watch it, girl, or you'll be smeared all over these fucking walls." The teenage lifeguard who, when she was six, blew his whistle, pointed, and yelled, "All the way back, and walk!" Old women whose voices splattered her when they told her what to do. Anyone who called her *honey*, *sweetie*, or *Miss Megan*. Anyone who used a leaf blower, psychotic bagpipes that roared her thoughts to bits. Anyone who made a noise over eighty decibels. If Megan had had her way, she would have murdered millions.

A flicker caught her eye, and she tensed in one red bootie and one black sneaker. Two slim dark threads broke the line where the stove's black rim met the white wall. They danced out of sync as they scanned the room like two tiny periscopes. Megan seized the stove and scraped it forward. The neighbors would think she was launching a noise campaign. A molasses-colored bug shot down the wall, and she looked wildly for a weapon. Not her books. Beside the door, neat pairs of shoes lay waiting for feet they hadn't housed in months. She grabbed a flesh-colored pump with a dense horseshoe heel. The roach dashed across the floor, and she stomped with her sneakered foot. The brown bug dodged and flattened himself where two walls met the floor.

He was a big guy, with plates that varied from amber to chocolate and serrated legs like black razor wire. Megan tried to dislodge him, but her curved shoe and sneakered foot couldn't reach him. She ran for the broom and found him again in the forest of chair and table legs. One swipe of her broom sent him flying, but he righted himself and ran. The dark creature zigzagged under the table, then charged her and scrambled onto her red bootie. Megan kicked wildly, and he hit the table leg and froze. Megan gripped her shoe.

In a deadly arc, she smashed the heel down, and his back split into three uneven pieces. His barbed legs flailed as he oozed brown juice. Megan hit him as though driving a nail. The man below would think she was throwing a tantrum, but the woman might sense the pattern in the bangs.

From then on, Megan killed every roach she saw. It shamed her to crush defiant life, but this life opposed her own. The co-op board said all the dryer vents were connected; she would have to work out the problem with her neighbor. Jenna expressed sympathy but seemed unconcerned. She knew of no companies that rerouted dryer vents.

In November, people voted the president out of office and streamed into the streets to dance. Megan stayed home and graded, fearing the virus would jump among buoyant people. In frames of a slow-rolling film, the red welts on her arm and leg faded and shrank. When she woke at three thirty to embrace Blount, she felt less fear of disgusting him. The bass of her neighbor's snores suddenly ceased, changing the texture of night sounds. Megan wondered what ailed him—hopefully not the virus. The missing continuo distracted her from her coupling with Blount.

The pandemic worsened, killing a thousand per day, then two thousand, and three thousand. She ventured out, masked, only to buy food or hurl her trash into the green dumpster. One morning, as she carried a straining bag, she saw her neighbor struggling with a laundry basket. Leaning against a dull silver car, the woman balanced her load on one hip as she dug for keys in a brown purse. As Megan approached, the woman's dark eyes widened with fear over her ribbed mask. She looked from side to side as though hoping the nearby cars would roar to life and save her.

"Can I help?" asked Megan.

She dropped the trash bag and offered her black-mittened hands. The woman clutched her green basket piled with folded shirts. Tears fell from her lowered eyes.

"I—I was just taking him some clean clothes," she said. "He's in the hospital. At Emerson."

Megan stopped with her arms extended. "I'm sorry. Is it the virus?"

The white-haired man had never worn a mask in their entryway.

"No, no!" sobbed the woman. "It's the cancer. That's why we're here. For the treatments. But something's happened. They have to keep him now." She shifted the basket on her hip and nearly dropped it.

"Let me hold that." Gently, Megan pulled the basket from her grip.

"Thank you."

The trembling woman dug a tissue from her purse, pulled down her mask, and blew her nose. Megan stepped back, gripping the green plastic rim.

"I can't stand seeing him like this," said the woman. "It

makes me sick—the things he said to you. So angry. That's not who he is. He's funny—and kind. And now …"

"Emerson's a great hospital," said Megan. "One of the best in the country. I'm sure they'll help him. I hope he gets better soon."

The woman rubbed a gray sleeve across her face so hard it must have hurt. "He's not going to get better." Her tears flowed. "They're talking about hospice care."

"I'm sorry." Megan's eyes were wet. "Let me—let me help you with this. Let's get him his clean clothes."

The woman lowered her eyes to her purse and this time found her keys. Megan slid the basket onto the gray backseat, which smelled of acrid dust.

"You're very kind," said the woman. "I—I'm so sorry. About everything."

"Don't worry," said Megan. "Let me know if I can do anything else."

Megan raised the black rubber lid of the dumpster and slung her bag full-force. It flew in a satisfying arc and smacked the rusty rear wall. The dingy silver car chugged by, and her neighbor waved. Megan paused, gripping the heavy black lid. George—that was his name. His passing was ravaging this poor woman, yet his last breath meant the death of a dictator, the resurgence of life.

Why would a woman spend her life waiting on one willful man? Reading one book in a world of wisdom? Tending one flower in a world of beauty? Lucy Blount had to serve her blond brood like a neglected, harried hen. She lived to fulfill needs that bourgeoned as her youngsters grew. Each time Blount was summoned by cruel calls, she rebuilt plans that had collapsed. In discount stores, she sought blue shirts that restored light to his eyes. Their tone had faded as he shuttled from his cubicle to their sheetrock home. His eyes had never glowed blue for her as they did when he was tracking a killer.

In the night, Blount stopped coming to Megan. His flat voice no longer stirred her dreams. When she awoke at three thirty, she raked the silence with her ears but found it had lost its form. Without George's snores, the night sounds had no pattern. They rose randomly and then quickly flopped: a gurgle from the restless refrigerator, a cough from a man on the street outside. Megan rubbed her legs together without fear that she would spread the rash. Her bumps had flattened to purple islands paler than her mangrove clumps of blue veins. She sensed Blount's longing as a tidal pull, but a stronger force held him in place.

Megan almost missed his knock: two faint taps, a rest, and two beats.

"Wichita PD!" he called through her red door.

Megan pulled it open, and there stood Blount. He entered as she backed away, as though a taut line connected them. Blount looked haggard, the curves under his eyes more deeply sculpted. His navy-blue work shirt darkened the shadows of his face. He stepped toward her with his hands extended.

"I came to check on you," he said.

"Thanks. I'm all right," she murmured.

Blount's pale blue eyes met hers. His full lips twitched.

"No," he said. "You're not, are you?"

With a sob, Megan fell forward to meet him. He embraced her, and she cried into his stale shirt.

"I don't want to hurt anybody." Her voice was a muffled blur. "I want to know you—be with you, but—"

Blount stroked her hair with a firm hand. "Why do you think I'm here? I might as well be. I'd be thinking of you wherever I was."

Megan swallowed and pushed herself free. "Walk away," she said.

Anguish seized Blount's pockmarked face.

"Walk away," she insisted. "You've done nothing wrong. Lying would kill you. I couldn't stand to see you hate yourself."

Blount gripped her shoulders until his fingers gouged. She thought he was going to shake her. Then his fingers relaxed, and his hands slid down her arms. He stepped back, turned, and closed the door softly behind him. Far off, the faint growl of his car scraped the night.

Blount drove. He rolled from her dense neighborhood of hedged condos to a floodlit east–west boulevard. The bright road cut the night like a runway, and he imagined himself shooting up, soaring into the black. In the dimly lit strip malls, dark lumps filled the doorways—men bunking down in the thirty-degree night. One bundled man pushed a shopping cart, determined to keep moving. Nothing stirred outside the wan motels whose signs beamed sad glows. Blount passed under the interstate and scanned the concrete vaults where the poorest slept. No anger stirred the shadowed heaps that night.

He curved north along the river where the darkness bred. Behind black trees, the river flowed—not pretty, brown and scarred by snags, but it rolled along. It did its job. He pulled into a parking strip, empty at this hour. No kids, come to make out or buy drugs. Blount cut the motor and reached into the glove compartment for a Snickers. Savoring each sweet, salty chew, he leaned back and closed his eyes. He could hear only his own mouth working, his own exhaled breath.

Amazing what the world could do. That he would find this woman at his age. Every cell in him cried out for her—to lie down with her, to merge. A strange woman, and none too young. That pain in her eyes had taken years to grow. And she didn't seem to mind her brother's death. Might even have set him up.

Blount bit off another hunk and shifted his back. He wouldn't think about that now. He'd think of how she looked so hungry, one touch of his lips would set her writhing. In bed, she'd do anything he wanted, things that had barely approached his mind. He closed his eyes and exhaled slowly. Yes, he would think about that.

The brown river wouldn't have frozen yet, its water

spilling slowly southeast. Down to the Gulf, toward Galveston, where it might find a beach someday. Lucy had promised they'd retire there, the stubbornest town in the world. Every few years, a storm smashed hell out of the Pleasure Pier, and every year, they rebuilt that joystick jutting out into the Gulf.

Mountains of life lay between them and Galveston. Lucy's parents were too demented to run their farm or know it was time to sell. His son Travis wanted to defund the police. He would defund the kid's allowance, he'd said. He needed to talk to his older girl, Kelsey, whom Lucy had caught reading teen questionnaires: "Is it infatuation, or is it love?" And Carrie—was she seven or eight now?—was angry because he hadn't read her story. Mixon trashed the place— that was normal at three, but it tired Lucy, and she cried. All four kids would need college, and they could barely pay their mortgage and eat. Extra shifts—all the work he could find. They hated him for being gone so much. And now he'd found this woman, a lost piece of his soul. Now, when, if he turned his head, he might run this rig off the road. Blount fingered his lips and tried to see the black trees. Their branches had dissolved into the night and wouldn't reemerge until dawn.

He should go home now and get some sleep before talking to the gang unit at nine. Not yet. Not just yet. He turned north and followed the black road across the river. Big box stores floated like palaces in dim lakes of light. The few cars in their lots clustered together for safety: signs of tired cleaning crews mopping floors; women and children trying to sleep without homes to shelter them. So many women needed protection—women with bruised cheeks, slashed arms. Women and children trying to hide from the men who'd become their worst foes.

Blount crossed under the ring road and passed Crystal Lake, a deep pocket of black. Light shone again in the town of Valley, then quickly died as the street narrowed to a county road.

Over the soybean fields hung the white hook of a new moon. The harvest had come in weeks ago, but some frozen plants were still standing. Soon they would fall to mush against soil so hard they would lie there like wrecks for months. Then, somehow, in May, green shoots would rise in hypnotizing rows.

The road ran straight as a plumb line, and Blount let his eyes close. He was rocketing through black, breathing, breathing. He gripped the wheel so he didn't dissolve. Ahead, the glow of Route 50 burned the black with an intensifying flame. He turned onto the highway and headed east, but even when he reached his home, no trace of dawn warmed the sky.

His dogs heaved themselves up to greet him and tensed at the strange smell he had absorbed. He nudged them aside and moved toward the couch, where Lucy was rising. She smoothed her squashed curls and pulled her pink terrycloth robe more tightly around her. She laughed at herself as she raised an arm to protect her eyes from the light.

"You were waiting for me?" he asked. "You shouldn't do that. You haven't done that in years."

"I had a feeling," she said. "A bad feeling. It was dumb. It's gone now. Can I make you some breakfast?"

Blount kissed her curls and breathed their sweet scent. "We got any of those round sausage patties?" he asked.

Lucy swatted his backside, and he smiled guiltily.

On her walk that morning, Megan fingered clusters of vermillion berries. A sharp new moon still shone over a world gone hard and clear. She taught her last class and read her students' research papers, written under quarantine. She found her eighteen-year-olds heroic and gave most of them As. As she typed, she could see no pink trace of the oozing slash across her arm.

No high D or burning sweetness rose from downstairs. In the past weeks, silence had prevailed. In Washington, the defeated president blustered, but the people's vote held. Three companies offered a virus vaccine, and ethicists formed a distribution plan. As a healthy Zoom instructor, Megan would be nearly last in line. She hoped Martin Blount would stand in front, an essential worker with hypertension. Still banned from Germany, Megan dug in for her first Aliketa solstice. She planned to watch TV and drink every move of Blount's lips.

That night, he and Braverman sat facing a suspect they'd found hiding in her aunt's garage. Witnesses claimed she had ordered a killing.

"Come on," said Braverman. "Tell us what happened."

"It's hard," the blurred-out woman replied.

Blount leaned forward to meet her eyes. "Only you can tell us your story," he said. "Are you gonna let someone else tell it?"

With soft steps, Megan crept forward. She raised her middle finger in Braverman's line of sight. The camera flitted between Blount and Braverman, and she tracked its rhythm. As she drew near, the screen crackled. A hundred hairs over her lips snapped to life. In an impulse, she kissed Blount's pockmarked cheek. He started and turned to Megan with a smile of sad delight.

CAT

An apple knew where it liked to lie. Sheila had only to listen to find the spot. Like people, fruits hoped to hide their flecks, their bird pecks, their shameful bruises. In their sloped bins, the Macs pressed together with force that grew with each downward row. Only the toughest dared stand beneath, the deep red ones with spotless sides. Customers grabbed for those first, thinking YourFood made the finest fruits hardest to snatch.

A rosy sour-sweetness drifted up from the half-filled crate of Macs. Sheila tightened her grip and savored cool hardness in each palm.

"Top," gasped a lopsided fruit in a high, frightened voice.

Jeff kept Sheila on produce because he knew she had magic hands. He didn't know about her ears, just the small red hands that always did what her ears told them. Sheila had power in her fingers, Jeff said. The Croatian guys could wheel out the crates, which her skinny arms could barely budge. But in the bins, only she could find each fruit's home so that they clustered close. With Sheila stacking, even the customers who pried deepest couldn't set off an avalanche. If anyone else filled the bins, fruits tumbled in minutes. Apples thudded to the floor, their red cheeks flattened by bruises. Wily onions rolled toward freedom, throwing off their protective scales. Sheila liked the work—her hands gripping hardness, her eyes drinking color. Each piece of fruit had its curves, its surprises, its secret shames.

She placed the scared apple in the top row and rubbed

her damp palm against her hip. Under her green apron, she found bone, and its hardness reassured her. Jeff would like her mosaic of red.

Jeff Ohara ran YourFood like a swivel-headed owl. From produce, he could see a broken jar on aisle six or a cart that had rolled into a driveway. With a homeless shelter just down the street, Jeff had plenty to do. All day long, hungry men roamed in, not so much to steal as to feed their eyes on bright boxes and gleaming jars. The security man stuffed in his uniform drove off drunks who settled on their benches like leaves. Jeff went himself to help junkies with needles bobbing in their arms. Once, he'd rousted a naked man curled in the dumpster with his arms locked around a bag of trash.

Jeff's moist black hair lay so thick the finest comb would glide through soundlessly. Elvis hair. Dracula hair. Gleaming hair with its own dark scent. Black eyes that shied away from nothing. Already a bit of belly. Half Japanese or something, Lourdes said. No white guy could be that hot.

Just as the apple in Sheila's hand tried to speak, a customer squashed its voice.

"You heard that too?" she asked a tall woman in aqua leggings.

The brown-haired woman she'd addressed frowned and slid her phone into her slack purse. She looked as though she'd come straight from the gym without even combing her damp hair. Sheila recognized the speaker, an aging cyclist who moved as though she'd locked her soul to the rack outside. In heat, cold, or pounding rain, she appeared in a tight red jacket and saggy black spandex shorts. Squashed by her helmet, her gray-brown hair called plaintively for a blonde recharge. The checkers hated her since each week, she explained how to pack her silver bike bags, as though they'd never seen her before. In the aisles, she sometimes joined conversations—or started them—with people who hadn't heard her soft approach. The words she aimed at other shoppers might have been the only ones she ever spoke.

Tight with mistrust, the brown-haired woman looked down at the skinny bike girl. The little cyclist might have been sixty, but she moved with the trepidation of a kid waiting to be scolded. Today, she'd annoyed the gym lady by parachuting into her private world. Like everyone who talked on her phone at YourFood, the woman in aqua seemed shocked to find that anyone could hear.

"Oh, you heard …"

The taut energy of the bike girl drove the tall woman's anger back.

"Yes, that yowling," the gym lady said. "I was telling my friend. Out there in the lot—some animal is suffering. It's horrible! He must be in such pain."

"Yeah, I heard that too," said the bike girl. "We should do something. Sounds like a voice from hell."

Jeff's radar pinged against their silver carts, which had aligned to block a produce aisle. His quick, heavy steps approached.

"Hey, ladies," he said. "Can I help you find anything?"

At the sight of Jeff, the women's tightness softened.

"Oh, we're fine," said the tall woman. "But—"

"There's an animal crying in the lot outside," said the bike girl. "A cat, I think. Yowling like somebody's tearing its tail off."

Jeff glanced at the half-empty crate of Macs. "Sheila," he said, "go see what that is."

Sheila laid the unheard apple next to the timid one in the top row. Pride warmed her. For the craziest jobs, Jeff wanted her. There was nothing she couldn't or wouldn't do.

Outside YourFood's glass doors, the August air felt thick enough to cut. In hot, wet waves, its steam strengthened the sounds it carried. Two rhythms behind her revealed that the gym lady and bike girl were following. They'd been right about the yowls, which were loud enough to rock the cars on their swollen tires.

The cat's cries overpowered the rattle of Lourdes, who was out in the lot, collecting carts. Sheila's ears found the source: a black Impala whose side was marred by silver scrapes. Beside it bent Curtis, a homeless guy who sometimes stuffed packs of Chips Ahoy! down his pants. Lourdes aimed her convoy of carts at the Impala as though shifting a battering ram.

"What's down there?" Sheila asked Curtis, whose drooping pants revealed brown flesh.

"Dunno," he said. "Cain't see nothin'. Sound like some cat see the devil, and he tryin' to scare him back where he come from."

"I've got a light on my phone."

The woman in aqua passed her iPhone to the bike girl, who dropped onto all fours and scanned under the car. Another yowl raked the air.

"God!" cried the gym lady, her eyes reddening. "He must have been hit. He must have gone down there to hide."

"Oh, he ain't hiding," said Curtis. "Sound like he want the whole world to know where he at."

The rattle of Lourdes's carts came to a quick halt.

"You found him?" she asked.

Lourdes had strong brown hands, thick black hair, and fierce eyes. Beside her, Sheila felt like an undercooked thing.

Still scanning, the bike girl had lowered herself onto her belly. "Oh!" she cried. "Something moved. Back by the rear tire."

"Let me try."

Sheila pulled the warm, hard phone from her hand. She lay on her belly and braced her left hand on hot asphalt. With her right, she steadied the dancing bar of light. In the thick darkness, two golden circles glowed. The yowls ceased.

"I see him," she muttered to the bike girl, who had climbed back up onto her hands and knees.

"Let's scare him out of there," said Lourdes.

"No!" cried the tall woman. "If he's hurt, it could kill him to move."

In her aqua leggings and jersey, she was starting to sweat. Her face had gone red and blotchy.

"Don't you try to haul him out," said Curtis. "That cat bad."

"How do you know?" asked the bike girl.

"Please help him," said the sweaty woman. "Can you get under there?"

Still gripping the phone, Sheila crept forward. She'd have to change her apron when she was done. She hoped the black smudges wouldn't wreck the stiff green. Above her, hot shafts and tubes lurked, ready to tear her up. A loop of hair caught on a jutting rod, and she winced as she tore some hairs loose. She rested her chin on warm asphalt. An acrid smell rose from the tar.

A few feet from Sheila's extended hand, a low hiss stirred the air.

"Catty-catty," she murmured. "Catty vrushka."

If she were a cat, she would like those sounds.

With her palm braced against rough warmth, she pushed herself forward. She laid down the light. Her reaching hand found clumped fur.

"Catty vrushka."

Tearing, gouging pain. An explosion of movement.

"He loose!" crowed Curtis.

"You got him!" cried the bike girl.

Sheila reached for the phone but, with her burning hand, could barely grip it. Unevenly, she shoved herself forward until her head emerged into the light. The gym lady took back her phone, and Lourdes pulled Sheila to her feet.

"Pero, ¡mírate!" said Lourdes. "¡Qué sucia estás! Looks like you been fucking a chimney sweep."

"How's the cat?" asked Sheila. "Which way did he go?" On her hurt hand, the fingers curled strangely.

"He ran that way." The bike girl pointed toward the dumpsters.

Curtis smiled, his white stubble stirring. "He fed up," he said. "He want us all to know. He want us all to know he here."

"That's no he. That's a she," said Lourdes. "Un desastre de gata."

Sheila rubbed her hand against her hip, and her palm came back smudged. A red ring with two rubies had risen on the mound between her thumb and wrist. The burn in her hand was blazing.

"He get you?" asked Curtis. "You ought to go wash that."

"You should see a doctor. Get a shot," said the bike girl.

Lourdes glanced toward two carts poised in a prime spot as though they were holding their heads together. She gripped the bar of her silver convoy.

"Ask Jeff for the day off," she said. "Go to a clinic."

Curtis ambled back toward the front benches. The bike girl and gym lady hurried into the store, the biker probably worried about her silver bags.

Sheila rushed for the back entrance, pulling her filthy apron from her as she ran. Any movement of her right hand caused echoes of the burning bite. She reached the restroom without being seen and scrubbed her face and arms with soapy paper towels. Her apron had borne the brunt of the abuse, but a black circle on her chin recalled Lourdes's thought. Who would ever want to lie down with her, a pale, badly formed thing? Her eyes and hair gave off no warmth, camouflaging a body whose back wouldn't grow straight. Sheila scoured until her skin turned pink and her white T-shirt and jeans were damp. The apron she threw into the laundry. Probably, whoever cleaned YourFood's linens had seen worse.

As she pushed through the bathroom door, she just missed hitting Jeff. A slight frown tautened his face, and he was breathing fast.

"I heard you got bit," he said. "Thanks for doing that. I didn't—"

"It's all right," said Sheila. "It's nothing."

"Let me see," said Jeff.

She raised her right hand, and he encircled her wrist, warm and solid. Jeff's breath stirred her hair.

"Mm," he murmured. "Oh yeah, I see it." Still grasping her wrist, he pulled her toward the pharmacy aisle. "Let's be sure," he said. "I don't want anything to happen."

Jeff drew her with a determined grip, and Sheila matched his steps. He seized a bottle of alcohol, a tube of cream, and some Band-Aids and pulled her toward the restroom.

"But this is the ladies'—"

"So let's shock 'em." Jeff grinned, his black eyes warming. "Hold out your hand."

Sheila gasped as cool liquid turned her hand to a torch

of icy flame. Jeff met her eyes and smiled and poured until the bottle was empty.

"Nothing too good for my best worker," he said. "That took guts, crawling under that car. That bike woman told me."

Jeff dried her hand gently and rubbed cream into the jeweled red ring. Her insides dissolved into warm waves. With strong fingers, Jeff pulled a Band-Aid taut.

"That ought to do it," he said. "You all right? You look like you're gonna faint."

"No. No," she murmured.

"Why don't you go home and rest?" he asked.

"Yeah," said Sheila. "Maybe I should. I just need to check produce."

"That's my girl."

Jeff enclosed her in a hug. She pressed into him, but her hand couldn't grasp his broad back.

"Hey, hey!" Jeff laughed and pushed her off. "We're working here."

He opened the door and glanced around quickly. No one saw Sheila emerge in his wake.

A cry from Luka sounded from produce, followed by a laugh from Maxamed. In between came a burst of soft thuds—an avalanche and then scattered impacts. Luka stood rigid with fear. Tall and dark, he had extended his long arms like a failed magician, trying to hold the apples back. Maxamed was bent double, chasing fruits that had flooded the floor.

Jeff rushed up as though he felt the avalanche in his own insides.

"Oh fuck," he muttered. "It's all right," he told Luka and Maxamed. "Let's fix this. Sheila, you're in charge. Do whatever she says. She'll teach you how to stack. First, let's get this aisle clear. Good work, Maxamed."

The thin-faced Somalian man looked up, shocked.

With her left hand, Sheila seized an apple, a tough green one that had refused to fall.

"C'mere, Luka," she said. "People like to pull from below. You gotta stack 'em so no matter where they pull, the apples hold together. Pick 'em up, and you can feel where they need to go."

Luka caught on faster than she thought he would, from the way his hands were shaking. With long, hairy fingers, he clutched the apples as though they were grenades. She showed him how to tell which fruits craved each other's shapes, how to sense their need to lie together. His hands stopped trembling as he studied their round forms, no two of them alike. While she straightened the pears, she let him stack. Then she tested his cobbled slope. When she pulled three fruits from the bottom, Luka's stack began to slide. Instinctively, he spread his arms and pressed his full body against the sloped bin.

"What are you doing to those apples, man?" Maxamed laughed but rushed to stop the fruits from falling.

"Keep trying. You're going to get it. You're doing better already," said Sheila.

She frowned at her hand, whose burn had sunk to a low flame as long as she didn't straighten her fingers. She left Luka trying to raise himself without letting an apple roll.

Sheila liked to leave through the back so that customers wouldn't see her. The reek of the dumpsters made her retch, but she paused at a scrambling sound in one whose mound had risen over its green sides. With a bound, the cat landed at her feet and crouched, staring up boldly. Sheila drew back her hands. With its back arched, its ears flat, the cat fixed her with golden eyes.

Lourdes had been right. The thin face was female, and the scrawny, dark thing seemed to know Sheila. Black, with a half-white nose and ragged ruff, she looked as though an angry artist had hurled paint at her. A plucked tail flicked over her matted back as she tensed, ready to spring.

"Catty vrushka," murmured Sheila, an incantation her mother had used to lure their cat from hiding when Gerald hit.

The cat sat back, erect, and curled her tail around her white paws. All the way across the lot, down Poncey Road to her apartment, Sheila felt the cat's yellow eyes tracking her.

She closed her locks, *click, click, click*, savoring the best minute of the day. This instant would be followed by the worst, since she hadn't cleaned herself that morning.

Better do it fast, she thought, so she'd be ready for dinner.

She cocked her right arm, drew a breath, and gave her cheek a burning smack. Her left arm answered, and a rhythm rose of lashing, searing flame. Down it burned, her hands tightening to fists, the smacks hardening to dense thuds. She stopped, panting, her face stinging, her right fist burning like a white coal. For a while now, she could feel clean. She had beaten the badness out.

Shaking, she settled onto her couch and brought her TV to life. Miserable eyes looked out at her. *Big* had started, a show about fat people desperate to lose weight. They lived in flat places without any trees, and when they gained, a plump doctor scolded. Sheila watched, amazed, as they devoured gooey pizzas and ordered their families to bring more. In time, some of them did shrink; others got fatter and cursed the doctor. Sheila loved the show for its sad music, which she liked to mirror on her keyboard.

"Sometimes I wonder why I'm here," said a seven-hundred-pound woman of twenty-four.

A soft blue-gray slide of tones. Sheila rose and snapped on her keyboard.

"My life is this room. I haven't been out in years."

Sheila tested a tone, and it matched. Clumsily, she doubled the descending blue line, keeping pace as the stream turned brown. Every press of a key caused a burn, the tune searing into her right hand.

As the fat people drove toward the doctor's city, the music settled on a rising phrase. Over and over, four sad, hopeful notes flowed along in a mud-brown stream. Sheila's mother had spoken of roads like that, lanes of cars rushing toward LA. They sped over swamps where gators lurked and sands where rattlesnakes slid. Her mother used to talk of the guys at Home Builders and her friends at Clark Community College. Drinking nights. Covering for Fred when he dropped boxes: "That lamp must have left the factory dented. Don't they ever inspect those things?"

Fred bought a car, a used midnight-blue Charger, and bragged he was driving to LA.

"Who'd you buy it off?" they jeered. "Some farmer who liked to ride around with his pigs?"

The engine rasped like a bear's snore. Crystal found a hole in the back floor. This wreck was going to cross a desert?

"Who wants to find out?" asked Fred. "I'll take as many as will fit."

Sheila loved the story of Fred and his snoring blue-black car. Her mother laughed, her face alight, as she described Crystal's face when her gold sandal broke through the mat and ground against rough asphalt. Her mother's light dimmed when the story ended in its own special night. Crystal agreed to go with Fred—if she could sit in front—along with the guys who'd scoffed loudest. Her mother stayed on at Home Builders and, for a while, in her classes at Clark. She never spoke the last line, which hung like an overtone. Sheila was growing inside her.

Once Sheila emerged, her mother stayed stuck like a girl on the roof of a flooded shack. You couldn't fault her for clinging when the brown water below might harbor whipping snakes. Better to watch the boats chug by and flag down the worthiest craft. Her mother kept working but stopped studying business and looked toward the men who veered her way.

The kindest left quickest. Mike used to crawl on the rug with Sheila until her mother told him to rise. He offered to drive them to the beach one day, and for an hour, they waited, straining to see his black truck shimmer where their straight street closed to a point. Mike didn't come, and after that day, they never saw him again. Her mother said he must have moved on to a new construction site.

After Mike came Harrison, who brought them ice cream in cold, tight-wrapped blocks. Sheila dreamed of building an igloo with the dense, frosty black boxes. When she peeled them open, she found peach or chocolate and once, on the Fourth of July, strawberry, vanilla, and blueberry. Harrison didn't shout, and his belly jiggled when he danced to his favorite song, "La Camisa Negra." Watching him bounce, her mother laughed on a high tone until his dance dissolved. Gradually, Harrison stopped coming, and Sheila wondered if her own bright laugh had scared him off.

Her mother never said that men decamped because she had a pale girl attached. Warm and shapely, Sheila's mother drew men like a rich forest with hungry ticks. Sheila caught their words when her mother batted them off so the phrases wouldn't splat in her own face. Owen, who ran the lumberyard, explained that after a few nights, he couldn't stay.

"If you want to move up," he said, "you can't take on

a woman with a kid. Only way they're going to pull you is down."

Unlike Owen, Gerald wanted a child.

"A woman should have children," he said.

It didn't matter that Sheila wasn't his. He felt as though he'd won the lottery: a brown-haired babe and a kid with no screams, no diapers, no shit. Gerald inspected construction sites and earned enough to ease her mother's fears. To make rent, they didn't have to play the dinner game, describing phantom foods they were devouring while the bare table reflected the TV's flickers. Gerald bought them matching checked dresses and said that in stores, people looked approvingly. He told her mother how he liked her brown hair—loose and wavy—and Sheila's—looped in tight braids.

One day Gerald brought home a kitten—a striped, half-blind, crawling thing. A stray had birthed a bunch of them at a building site, and the guys had divided the mewing furballs among them. The kitten seemed to know who had rescued her and rubbed his feet the minute he came home.

"See? That's loyalty," he said, his fingers following stripes down the cat's head. "Wish some other people around here would show that kind of appreciation."

Gerald wanted appreciation at night, because that was when his voice rose. Sheila woke to hear him shouting at her mother, who seemed to have done something wrong.

"I'm sorry," she said in a voice that hardly dared stir the air.

In the morning, she moved jerkily until Gerald sped away. Once he left, she sometimes found her laugh, but Gerald always came home. He stayed until the cancer ate her mother up when Sheila was seventeen.

Unlike her mother, Sheila had little to fear from men. Her curved back and pale, pinched face drew curiosity at best. Men noticed the things she did, not her looks, for which a few could forgive her. Jeff had praised her for scraping a dried-out rat from under a storage bin. She'd had to crawl down under there too and locate the body by the smell. Jeff told her she was lean and agile. In the night, those words spun round, raising smoke when they rubbed together. She rolled onto her belly and circled her hips.

"I like how you handle yourself," Jeff murmured.

Sheila drew her tingling hand under her. That smile in Jeff's eyes as he poured. She brought her lips to his neck, and his breath caught. The black scent of his hair filled her.

"Don't leave me," he whispered. "I want you with me always."

He pulled her to him, and this time, when they merged, he didn't push her away.

Strangely, Jeff didn't drive off the cat. Usually, he freaked if a four-legged creature breached the dumpsters. But this cat could kill vermin, he said. Better cats than coons. This scrawny thing might not look like much, but to a mouse, it was Godzilla. And it spared the customers, didn't return to the lot. The cat seemed to like the trash. Harapos, Lourdes called it—Rags, the ugliest cat she'd ever seen. On break, she slipped it pricey food in silver tins with an Egyptian cat goddess on them.

Sheila found the bright cans licked clean, even under the rims of their rounded corners. She pictured a pinkish tongue expertly catching the last crumbs of meat. Since the day of yowling, no one had seen Harapos, but Sheila sensed the force of her golden eyes. She might be lowering in some crevice, with bags pressing her bony sides. As Sheila tossed a tin over the dark green wall, she aimed for the least likely spot.

With a soft crack, the tin struck the side and fell to the dry asphalt. Sheila rubbed her hot hand against her thigh and reached for the silver square. A soft sound startled her, and she felt a light touch against her thigh. There stood Harapos, her twitching tail forming fleeting black question marks in the air.

The cat blocked Sheila, weaving around her legs, as she walked toward Poncey Road. She felt heavy in the heat after hours of grabbing fruit Luka and Maxamed had dropped. Jeff had put her in charge of produce, and she had to train them without slowing the roll from crates to bins. Despite Jeff's bath of fire, her hand stung, and sticky drops oozed where the rubies had darkened. She had planned to go to a clinic that night, but she longed for her keyboard, her couch. If she had to undress, a doctor might ask about the bruises blooming on her thighs. Better to let her hand heal itself. Harapos was herding her toward home. The cat rubbed her thin jowls against Sheila's jeans until Sheila nearly fell.

64

"What do you want, cat?" she asked.

The black-and-white face looked up, blank. The rough fur did not invite petting. Sheila walked on, and Harapos resumed her nudging interference.

The cat wound her way through Sheila's space, rubbing her scuffed door, her white stove, her blue couch with patchwork pillows. Harapos's ears flattened when the locks snapped, but nothing broke her liquid motion. For dinner, Sheila topped some gold crackers with rosy rounds of salami. She loved circles within circles: a stoneware plate of crisp rounds rooved by disks crammed with red-and-white blobs. Harapos kept her eyes on the meat, breathing its spicy, sour scent. Sheila tossed her a round of salami, and a white tooth flashed as she tore it up.

Sheila brought the TV to life, and the room filled with sad sound.

"Everything hurts," said a huge woman whose belly flowed like lava.

Big had given the woman her own melody, or maybe the tune was her thought. The song reached up and sank in blue steps. Sheila found the first note on her keyboard, a white one flanked by two blacks. A fireball burst in her hand as the smoky blue tone sounded. When she reached for the high note, her tone scraped against the poor fat woman's song. Sheila pulled back her hand. Harapos glanced up from the coffee table, where she had cocked her head to chew.

When the melody cycled back, Sheila reached again for the high tone. This time, she matched its clear blue but only because she used her eyes. She could see the right key, but the bent finger seeking it fell short. She stared at her hand and tested her fingers, playing a ghost scale in the air. Her limp fingers moved more slowly than they should have, as though they were stunned or half asleep. How stupid! How useless! She couldn't even use her own hands.

Something burst, and she smacked her cheek with all the strength in her hurt hand. Pain exploded. Which side was stronger? The stinging burns said they were evenly matched. On the dark table, Harapos ate faster, dipping her head to gulp larger bites.

Sheila stood slack, her arms hanging at her sides. She turned off her keyboard and sank onto the couch. Harapos jumped to the brown carpet. She had left a plate of crisp gold rounds, indented circles on a pale moon. On each cracker, six piercings formed a tight ring around a central hole.

At YourFood, Lourdes told Sheila she was worried. For the past two days, she'd found tins of congealed food whose oily surfaces had been broken only by mice. Sheila had to tell her that Harapos had found a better gig.

Lourdes's plucked eyebrows rose. "You're feeding that thing? ¡Qué carajo! After she tried her teeth on your arm?"

"Yeah, I think she likes me," said Sheila.

"She likes *food*," said Lourdes. She threw the silver tin of gelled meat into the dumpster.

Curtis wandered over from the bench where he'd been

greeting customers in his gravelly voice. His hand shook as he pointed at Sheila.

"How that hand?" he asked. "You see a doctor yet?"

Sheila rubbed her burning wrist against her jeans. Her hand left a sticky smear on the tight cloth. The bump under her thumb looked redder and fatter than the mound on the left-hand side.

"I can't believe you didn't go," said Lourdes. "We're going today."

She looked with disgust toward the bike rack, where the bike girl was unlatching her silver bags. The determined woman plunked them down and groped for her lock, her mushroom rump in the air. Lourdes aimed an imaginary kick that would have sent her sprawling over the steel rack.

Inside, Jeff stopped to speak with the bike girl but welcomed Sheila only with a faint nod. Since he'd touched her, he had veered away like a pebble that had struck glass.

Sheila wrapped herself in a green apron and looked at the fruit she'd have to stack. Maxamed smiled and waved as he wheeled in cartons of Bartlett pears. Pears were tricky, so Sheila asked Maxamed to check the vegetables when he was through.

"Put the prettiest part out," she said, "so if your mother shopped here, she'd find them all so beautiful she couldn't choose."

Maxamed laughed in a rasping tone that Sheila had come to like. His thin face glowed, but she couldn't read his thoughts as he pictured his mother shopping at YourFood.

Lately, customers hadn't been buying many Bartlett pears. Their pale green couldn't compete with the peaches' purple-and-orange sunset. Sheila would have to move the stacked pears—sweet, yellow, thin-skinned—and rearrange them over the hard green pears from that day's crates. No two pears had the same shape, and when she breathed the new batch's bittersweetness, she saw green bells, blobs, bumpy lightbulbs. To lay a sloped, cobblestoned bed of these would take ingenious hands.

Sheila set to work, moving the sweet, tender-skinned pears so she could build the crocodile skin on which they'd lie. She was learning to grip with three stiff, curled fingers, using the outer two as a clamp. The green pears must have been chilled, because a fine moisture had made them slick. She grabbed one that looked like a candle—thin top, wick stem—and it shot from her hand and bounced over the white floor. Ashamed, she stooped to pick it up, and two more dropped alongside. Sheila slowed her pace, laying pears as though assembling a green jigsaw puzzle.

Luka and Maxamed walked up, laughing at some joke they had shared. Tall and slim, with the same long arms, they had begun to bond, although they moved differently.

"What should we do now?" asked Maxamed. "You need any help with those?"

"No," said Sheila. "Go see what else we should bring out."

With her left hand, she wedged the last two pears into tight spots. Thanks to their slickness, they slipped in. Before the first buyers came on their way to work, she wanted the ripe, tender pears up top. In a day or two, they'd soften to brown mush, and she meant to give them every chance. What a life—hanging on a tree, then stifling in a box, only to rot in a stinking dumpster.

Even though the ripe pears were warm, they felt slippery too. A sweet yellow pear slid from her grasp and fell with a splat, disconsolate. The new pears below must have made it wet, since the store felt anything but cool. Sheila held the spoiled pear to her face, which was glowing hot enough to grill it. Carefully, she placed more pears in the hard green hollows of her slope. Only a few more needed homes.

Voices flashed through an uneven rattle—Luka and Maxamed wheeling out a fresh load. She laid a big, browning pear in back, and her curled fingers caught the stem of a pear below. The slope came alive, rolling free like an escaping herd. Sheila spread her arms, hugging the pears as Luka had, but she lacked his wingspan. An explosion of thuds sounded, hard and angry, soft and pained. Rushing steps approached—more than Sheila could count.

Strong arms pulled her from the pears as she fought and cried, "No!"

The bin had emptied except for a green cross of fruit pinned by her body and arms. Maxamed saved a few pears, but most had dropped to join their friends on the white tiles.

Jeff was holding Sheila firmly with no fondness in his touch.

"What's wrong with you?" he hissed in her ear. "It's just fruit. We've got customers."

Jeff shook her before he released her.

"Bring a trash can—a big one," he told Luka. "Nothing on the floor goes back on that pile."

In a different tone, he addressed the bike girl, who was grabbing pears as though she could keep all she caught in thirty seconds.

"No, ma'am, please don't do that! It's our job. Our mistake."

The bike girl turned her dirty-blonde head and smiled. "Free pears?" she asked mischievously.

"Nope." Jeff matched her tone like a singer. "We're taking these out of circulation."

He lowered his voice and said to Sheila, "Go home. See a doctor. You're not well."

He guided her left hand toward the bin and pried her fingers from a pear they were crushing to pulp.

Poncey Road led to the Grove County Clinic, which had seized a dark strip mall a few years back. Sheila remembered the mildew smell from when she'd bought shirts there, so the air-conditioning must have survived the move. She felt grateful to the tired, chugging HVAC for making the room full of bodies bearable. Lourdes's voice helped too, like a fond rub that sought no answering touch. For five hours, she addressed everyone waiting and shared peanut butter cookies from the vending machine.

Lourdes stuck so close to Sheila that when they finally went in, the young Black doctor hesitated, glancing between them. Sheila held up her hand, and the doctor focused her gaze, as though she could heal the bite by staring. With deft fingers, she probed and pulled. She whipped back her hand when fluid squirted even though she was wearing gloves.

"A cat bit her," said Lourdes. "A really bad cat. From the dumpster."

Her words sounded unfair to Harapos.

"She was protecting herself," said Sheila. "I was trying to grab her."

"When was this?" asked the doctor. Despite her weariness, she tensed. She looked toward Lourdes, whose full lips were moving.

"Cinco ... seis—about a week."

"And you're coming in *now*?"

The doctor fixed her strong eyes on Sheila's. Behind her round glasses, her eyes beamed searing questions.

"I had to work," said Sheila. "I had to take care of the cat."

A whoosh of air expressed Lourdes's disgust. The doctor's gaze didn't waver, but her eyes reddened. She snapped off her soiled gloves and pulled on a fresh pair.

"Take off your things," she said. Her voice hit a bump but kept rolling. "I'd like to look you over."

Sheila pulled her shirt over her head. She fumbled with the silver button on her jeans, which kept sliding from her fingers.

"Let me help you," said the doctor.

Up close, the dark woman had a runner's intensity. The

jeans slid down, and the doctor froze, gripping tight cloth. Nightmare flowers covered Sheila's thighs—blue-black, yellow, rust-green.

"Que la chingada," whispered Lourdes.

"Who's hitting you?" asked the doctor.

She released her grip and straightened up so close that Sheila inhaled her warm breath.

"No one," said Sheila.

The doctor sought Sheila's eyes, but Sheila kept them on her blue bruises.

"If it's a guy—a partner—we can help," said the doctor. "There are hotlines. Women's shelters."

"It's not a guy," said Sheila.

"She's telling the truth." Lourdes cut in. "She doesn't have a boyfriend. She doesn't date. She stays alone mostly."

"Someone did this." The doctor circled her fingers over the bruises so that she wouldn't cause pain with her touch. "I can't make you call the police, but I should report this."

"She doesn't have to say if she doesn't want to, does she?" asked Lourdes.

"No." The thin doctor exhaled slowly. "Sheila, would you please look at me?"

Sheila kept her head down. If she looked into the dark eyes again, tears would flow.

"You did this to yourself, didn't you?" The doctor's voice rose on a wave. "This and not coming in after that bite—you know you could die? This is a bad infection. Your tendons may be severed. I don't know if we can save your hand—get it back its full function."

Sheila drew her hand to her breast. On the doctor's thin face, anger dissolved into sadness.

"You need to go to the hospital," she said. "Right now. I can call for a transport, or you can go yourself—that's cheaper. But you have to go. You could die."

Still tense, she turned to Lourdes. "Can you take her there? Really—can you make her go?"

"Yeah. We'll go," said Lourdes.

Sheila pulled up her jeans. She breathed in sharply as her reaching fingers set off bursts of pain.

"Espera. Yo te ayudo," murmured Lourdes.

The doctor stepped back to let Lourdes fasten Sheila's silver button.

Lourdes took Sheila to Emerson Hospital, which was closer than County Hospital downtown. In the hot, wet night, its glass walls gleamed behind closely spaced streetlights. As Sheila lay in the ER, machines beeped and flashed, and she felt like an experimental animal on an alien ship. A burn was building on her lower arm where clear fluid flowed in through a tube. Tears slid from the corners of her eyes, tickling as they rolled toward her ears. Lourdes gripped Sheila's left hand. Her right had been cleansed, muffled in white, and splayed out on some sort of tray.

With a warm finger, Lourdes caught a tear as it crept down toward Sheila's hair.

"No llores," she whispered.

"I can't pay for this," murmured Sheila. "They'll take my wages. I'll lose my apartment. I'll be on the street."

"You have insurance." Lourdes pressed her hand. "Everyone at YourFood does. It sucks, but it'll cover some. And this place—they want to study you here. Maybe they'll give you a discount."

Sure enough, in the next hours, doctors of every rank squinted at the peeping consoles and frowned at Sheila's wrapped hand. Their faces shifted like chips in a kaleidoscope, and Sheila closed her eyes to stop the dizziness. In the darkness, she tried to interweave their flying scraps of voice.

"Get the fever down … animal control … put down …"

Sheila gripped Lourdes's hand and tried to pull herself up.

"¿Qué haces? ¡Cálmate!"

Lourdes pushed her back down.

"They want to kill her!" said Sheila. "She's in there all alone. They're going to find her."

"What are you talking about? You've got a fever. They say your fever is high. No one is going to kill anyone. Try to rest."

"No!" Sheila tried to raise herself without Lourdes's help. "Harapos. They want to kill Harapos. She's at my place. She has nothing to eat."

"Menos mal."

Lourdes's lips twisted. Sheila opened her eyes, and Lourdes's round face shimmered over her.

"Take my keys," said Sheila. "Take her to your place. They won't find her there. She likes salami."

"Ni de broma," said Lourdes. "Are you crazy? I'm not touching that thing. You want me to end up here with you? Is that it?"

"Then let her out," whispered Sheila.

A black-haired nurse scowled as she walked by.

"You don't have to touch her. You could just go, leave something to eat outside …"

"Mira."

Lourdes sat back and closed her eyes. She shuddered as though a snake had slid through her. Her dark eyes opened to reveal hidden hardness.

"I won't feed that cat until you stop hitting yourself," said Lourdes.

Sheila found herself floating in a hot bath of shame.

Lourdes leaned in. "I won't take your fucking keys. Pero, ¡qué locura! What pimp has contracted his beatings out to you? What fool is guiding your hands?"

"No one." Sheila's whole body burned. "I just hate myself sometimes."

Lourdes exhaled in a whoosh. "Somebody made you hate yourself. You ever see a baby hit itself—on purpose?" She smiled. "Kids hit everyone *but* themselves. Some asshole taught you to beat yourself so he wouldn't have to do it."

Sheila's voice dissolved in a wet wave. "It makes up for the badness."

"Mierda." Lourdes squinched up her lips. "People who should be beaten for badness, you're way down the list. And beatings just make you badder." She seized Sheila's left hand. "You have to swear. You don't have any kids—any family. I know! Swear on the eyes of our fat boss. Swear you'll never hit yourself again, or that cat starves."

"I swear," said Sheila.

The promise took no work to give. Since the day she'd botched the fat woman's song, Sheila had felt no more urge to hit.

The black-and-silver console shimmered as though she were gazing into a tank.

"You should go home. You're tired," she told Lourdes. "I'm sorry. I promise. So you'll let her out?"

"Yeah." Lourdes's voice settled. "Or she'll claw your place to confetti."

Sheila's eyes closed. She sensed Harapos circling in the dark, settling at last on her bed.

The university doctors kept Sheila in the hospital, draining plump plastic bags into her arm. With a mouth like a saber-toothed tiger, Harapos had raked three tendons with one bite. Sheila's tough cords were holding, so the doctors gave her a brace and said they'd wait to see if her tendons healed. If her extensors couldn't grow back together, they'd have to cut her open and stitch them up. First, she had to fight off the *Yersinia*, cousins of the bacteria that had caused the bubonic plague. Sheila didn't have rabies, but Harapos's teeth had planted germs that could turn flesh to black ooze.

Sheila pictured a money meter on her console, registering hundreds, then thousands of dollars. As Lourdes predicted, a dozen doctors questioned her, and Sheila did her best to please them. Maybe if she volunteered for their studies, they would reduce her bill. One old Indian teacher sounded a lot like the scolding doctor on *Big*. He led in a group of tense, concerned students whose faces hung like a cluster of daisies.

"A cat did this," he said. "One bite. Healthy young woman, a week without antibiotics."

The students nodded and stared, some with sympathy but most with amazement.

Doctors and nurses probed Sheila's fingers, and their questions gravitated toward a central void. When she'd seen her hand weaken, redden, and ooze, why hadn't she come in sooner? Sheila tried to tell a sane story, since one digging doctor seemed fixed on her mind.

Not even the psychologist asked her about the hitting. Maybe the clinic doctor hadn't told; maybe her message had drowned in rapids of communications. Sheila's blue-and-yellow bruises lurked under the white blanket. Her wrapped hand drew a spotlight that left the rest of her body dark. With all the work these doctors had to do, why fix someone dumb enough to beat herself?

The doctors seemed hurt—angry even—that with her hand, she'd scorned what they had to give. Sheila told them she needed to work, but no one had made her stay away. From the moment the first needle had stung her arm, Sheila had worried about Jeff. Her story hid his fire bath like a forbidden light that mustn't be seen. Her manager had told her to see a doctor. No one had forced her to work—or to grab a stray cat. She had just misjudged the situation. This whole plague infection was her fault.

Jeff came to see her early the first morning, carrying a purple-and-orange bouquet. His eyes scanned the small room where they had moved Sheila but kept glancing toward the door. His glossy hair shone, and his belly tautened his white shirt. When he stroked Sheila's hair, a warm wave rolled through her.

"I'm glad you're OK," he said. "I had no idea it was this bad."

"I'm sorry," said Sheila. "I'm sorry I didn't go sooner. I'm sorry I messed up that fruit."

Jeff's gaze flickered, then recovered its warmth. "It's just fruit," he said. "We expect to lose some."

She raised her bandaged hand. Someone had stolen her real one and replaced it with this stiff white starfish.

"What if …" Sheila looked toward her wrapped fingers.

"You're going to get better," said Jeff. "This place is cutting edge."

"Will my insurance cover it?" asked Sheila.

Jeff looked toward the window. "Our insurance is good." His black brows pulled together.

"What if my share is more than I can pay?" asked Sheila.

"It'll cost something." Jeff rubbed a palm against his thigh. "But I'll advocate for you. With management. You can have as many shifts as you want."

Jeff met her eyes, and his gaze intensified, warm with threadlike currents of cool.

"It'll be fine, I'm sure," she said. "You'd better go back now."

Jeff's smile spread. "That's my number-one worker," he said. "One hand or two—who cares?"

Lourdes returned that night after a double shift. Her eyes were bright, though she could hardly have slept in days. She waited, compressing a laugh, while a tense Asian student changed Sheila's IV.

"Did you find her?" asked Sheila as soon as he left. "Was she hungry?"

"It wasn't easy," said Lourdes. "Felt like stalking a terrorist."

"Where was she?"

A black box on the console peeped faster.

"Damned if I know. I looked everywhere and couldn't find her."

"So she's still in there?" Sheila breathed quickly.

"Uh-uh." Lourdes shook her head, and her black hair bounced. "That's when I pulled out the meat. Put it on the steps and backed up toward the sidewalk."

"And she came out?" Sheila's face felt hot.

Lourdes nodded. "Like some ratty, beat-up ghost."

"What did—"

"Chorizo." Lourdes smiled. "I think she swallowed it whole. Then she took off down Poncey Road. But I'll find her. I'm going to check up on you. One bruise, and that cat dies, pinche gata del diablo."

In three days, Sheila's fever cooled. She had nearly torched herself battling bugs the cat had implanted. The pointy teeth had pierced and then withdrawn, embedding aliens that grew recklessly. The lusty things had lurked so deep that Jeff's burning bath hadn't touched them. Medicine in the plump bags had killed them off, and now it was time to see if her ripped tendons would mend.

Doctors unwound the bandages on Sheila's hand and sent her home with a brace. With black Velcro encasing her wrist, she felt like a cyborg. For weeks, she rested; then she returned to the hospital, where a low-voiced therapist told her to stretch her fingers. The thin outer two of her right hand obeyed, glad to show off what they could do. But the middle finger, index finger, and thumb lay curled, stiff, frightened, and stunned. Frozen between a clench and a stretch, they seemed ready to give up moving altogether and work instead as claws.

"Keep working," urged the husky-voiced therapist. She leaned in until her black hair tickled Sheila's cheek. "The tendons are damaged, but people underestimate therapy. Human bodies can survive all kinds of hurt. If you want your hand back, make it do everything it can."

At home, Sheila watched *Big* all day, smiling faintly when

the doctor chided. She hummed the show's deep blue and brown melodies, which fell when swollen people cried in their beds and rose when they drove to the doctor's clinic. With her pinkie, Sheila punched on her keyboard, but held by a black corset, her right hand couldn't shape the tunes' flow. She tried with her left but couldn't keep up. Her left fingers jumped in but then froze in panic, like kids given a grown-up job.

Matching melodies merely led the list of tasks Sheila's right hand couldn't do. She discovered she had used both hands to comb her hair, which formed a seaweed mass after a shower. One hand had clamped while the other had combed, shifting their holds as she raked through mats. Miserably, she asked Lourdes to chop off her hair, and Lourdes sent a friend who tried a pixie cut. In the mirror, Sheila saw a shaggy boy, but better that than a knotted nest.

The first time she went out for a walk, she found she needed two hands to get back in. Without realizing it, she had pulled the door toward her when she turned the last lock, the way you synced clutch and gas on an old car. If she didn't pull, the key wouldn't turn, and her keys clattered down three times before she learned to turn with her left hand and yank with her right.

Sheila's left hand had lagged in its learning, pleading dumb, while the right supplied the skill. Her left fingers had passed for having smarts they lacked, like a sister hired for nepotism rather than merit. Suddenly in a position of power, her left hand waffled, promoted too fast. At times, it seemed willing but clumsy; at others, hesitant to respond at all.

All day, Sheila tried moving her fingers in all the ways they used to spread. She fanned them, crossed them, extended them like feet, and dipped her "toes" down one by one. Recreating the therapist's low voice, she told her fingers they wouldn't move if they didn't try. But her right hand had become a different tool, a fulcrum or rake, not a grabber. The fixed curl of her three big right fingers defied all her attempts at straightening. She could no more flatten them out than Harapos could have turned her curved claws to spikes.

As Sheila played air keyboard and watched fat people eat, she wondered where Harapos could be. Lourdes brought supplies but reported no sightings. The lot and the dumpsters were clear. Jeff had brought in animal control after some tense calls with senior management. The police came with nets, but only rats jumped out when they banged on the green steel walls. Animal control left tins of poison they said tasted like steak and would kill anything on four legs.

Sheila's pulse quickened.

"She'd never eat it. She's too smart," said Lourdes.

Sheila wasn't so sure. If Harapos were hungry, with all the rats gone, what flesh would her saber-teeth tear?

Sheila pictured her black tail flicking, free to form any shape in the air. Stripped and skinny, that tail had suffered, but Harapos moved it with skill. A tail needn't float as a fluffy plume to bring a body grace. If Sheila had a tail, she would wave it angrily to warn off tall attackers. When she was alone, she would wrap it around herself for comfort.

If she were with Jeff, she would wind it around his legs, caressing him until he laughed. A tail might compensate for this cyborg hand that made her feel less alive.

In time, Sheila's thick fingers eased their curl like three long, eroding hills.

"Your tendons are mending," said the smoky-voiced therapist. "I don't know how. Think of a stretched rubber band hanging by a string, the torn parts finding each other and bonding. Your hand must really want to work."

Sheila smiled, proud of her shredded strings eager to grow back together.

Even before her right hand healed, Jeff urged her to return to YourFood. The chain prided itself on hiring the disabled, and Jeff said she would make a good greeter. Only Win-Mart had greeters, old people starving on Social Security who welcomed customers to their stores. With Sheila's help, YourFood could lead, showing what a greeter could bring to a midsize supermarket. Sheila knew the shelves, and with her help, people making strategic strikes could find their targets. Jeff didn't mention her looks, but she sensed they formed part of his plan. A hot greeter would make customers hate their bodies just as they were going to buy food.

Lourdes also begged Sheila to come back, saying she missed their talks. She trusted no other ears with her mutinous words, which would be heard but stray no further.

"You should sue," Lourdes told Sheila one night when

she stopped by after her shift. "That's what's scaring him. He's cute when he's scared—those black eyes get so big. I think his belly's shrinking."

Lourdes cupped her hands over her waist, then lowered them, miming a child's misery. Sheila joined in her laughter and was surprised to feel it come from such a deep place. Lourdes peeled down Sheila's jeans and nodded grudgingly when she saw only fading flowers.

"One new bruise," she said, "and I blacken those sexy eyes, just when Panzón is trying to help you."

According to Lourdes, Jeff was hounding management to pay everything Sheila's insurance wouldn't cover. He didn't say he'd told her to grab a cat on store property, but Lourdes had overheard "show of support" and "compassionate gesture." Sheila prayed Jeff would succeed, since notices tracking her costs said they came to $37,342.55. "This is not a bill!" began the shotgun sprays of numbers. The insurance company was calculating her share. Even a fraction of that killer sum would keep her from making rent.

"You should sue YourFood," said Lourdes. "You could get a whole lot more."

Sheila imagined Jeff's tight voice as he pleaded. He was fighting for their store but also for her. The next day, she offered herself as a greeter. Jeff hugged her until his thick body engulfed her. Her bent back didn't bother him, even when his warm fingers pressed her curve. Jeff wanted her for the look in her eyes that said how much YourFood mattered.

Before starting work, Sheila looped through the aisles, mapping celery, cream cheese, and Pampers. The learning thrilled her, since only Jeff could open the map in his head and see every curve and color. Now they would share these mosaic paths, where they could meet in their minds.

"Welcome to YourFood," intoned Sheila. "Can I help you find anything?"

She sought the right melody for each troubled person who rushed or drifted through the doors. Most dodged her the way they steered around the plastic goat on a bin of pungent soap. Some people smiled nervously, unable to ignore a fellow human who had addressed them. Others asked questions: "Where are the dog leashes? Where is the roach spray? The cilantro? Does YourFood have gluten-free cupcakes?" In English spliced from strange melodies, they asked for batteries, car wax, and cassava.

"Keep a list," Jeff told her. "Anything we don't have we can order. Thank them for bringing it to our attention. Say that if they come back in a week, we should have it—unless it's something totally weird."

In most cases, Sheila could send the tense people to the shelf warmed by her mind's light. She gave them landmarks as well as numbers: "Aisle nine, just under the water filters. If you hit the protein bars, you've gone too far."

After a few hours, her melodies felt mechanized. She began to wonder how her sounds made meaning. A burn was growing in her lower back, rising like noise in a packed room. The pain hid when she shifted her feet, then reappeared with increased boldness. Her hands longed for action, so she played tunes on her thighs. Her three stiff fingers were regaining strength.

After a week of greeting, Sheila asked Jeff if she could work in produce again. He scanned her from cropped head to tight sneakers.

"I like you as a greeter," he said. "But if you feel up to it, you can try."

Maxamed now ran produce with help from Luka and nervous Drago. Maxamed asked her to check the stacks, and her fingers welcomed smooth plums and dusty potatoes. She set to work arranging the plums, placing them on top when their softness pleased, tossing them when they gave beneath her fingers. She missed their fluty alto voices, which today her fingers couldn't hear.

With the plums, her hands' deafness didn't matter; they clung together like purple drops. But when she moved to the apples, she hesitated. Her awakening fingers fondled and squeezed, but the apples wouldn't talk. Maybe they distrusted her for leaving them; maybe the drugs that had killed the plague had zapped her powers. She didn't know where to put the red and green balls that had suddenly turned mute. Were they punishing her with their silence, or were they speaking to hands that couldn't hear? Her gripping fingers couldn't sense their wishes, only cool, round stillness.

After a day, she told Jeff and Maxamed it was no good. Her hands should work where they could do less harm.

Jeff assigned her to the pet food aisle, which each day saw battering action. Rail-thin Drago helped her wheel out cartons that held armies of meat-filled cans. With reviving fingers, she deployed them on the shelves, face forward, dust-free, ready to sing.

But oh! Each can sang with the same metal voice, unwavering, unfeeling, programmed. The Egyptian cat goddess's soprano differed from the dog food's bass, but their tones lacked the life to harmonize. Tears brimmed in Sheila's eyes. The gleaming cans might as well have been mute. Here she had no decisions to make. Each cylinder made the same sounds because each one had the same shape.

A puff of breath brushed Sheila's neck, and she turned to find the bike girl watching. The wiry woman was hunting— for what? Her cart held little more than her bike bags, but she hungrily searched each aisle.

"How's your hand?" she asked. Her eyes scanned Sheila's fingers.

"Doing the job," said Sheila.

"Have you seen that cat?" asked the bike girl. "Last week, I saw it perched up on the dumpster like a gargoyle."

Sheila's heart pumped a double beat. "You saw her?"

"Oh. Is it a she?" The skinny woman rolled her cart forward and back. "Well, she's around. I wouldn't touch her, though. I think she wants to eat but not let anyone near her."

The bike girl rolled away, her silver bags braced at a secure diagonal.

Jeff came often to check on Sheila, praising her can choirs, asking after her hand.

"We're wasting you here," he said one day. "You were great on produce, but you rocked as a greeter. You should see what's happening online."

In Sheila's week as a greeter, customers had posted their appreciation.

"An English-speaking human who knows the store," wrote one. "Who does that? I thought I was hallucinating, but the Drano was right where she said."

"My son's birthday party was in an hour," wrote another, "and she knew where the candles were."

Senior management had called. They wanted to launch a greeter program and shoot a training video with Jeff and Sheila. Jeff said he would do it if YourFood paid Sheila's medical bills. Would she join him? Yes, said Sheila. She would do it if Lourdes could costar. YourFood needed to show that they spoke Spanish.

Anytime Lourdes had a shift, Sheila called her to help people she couldn't understand. Phrases with a circular rhythm flowed from anxious mothers and men in paint-flecked clothes. When they spoke, they looked into Sheila's eyes so their gaze could help her absorb their meaning. Most of the dark, sturdy people strode by without speaking, but those with questions made her feel ashamed of her ignorance. With Lourdes, they bonded like birds happy to find others who sang the same song. Sheila wished someone were as glad to see her as the workers to spot Lourdes's round face.

Sheila didn't like her work as a greeter, since her strengthening hand had nothing to grasp. Between customers, she rubbed her hipbones and played tunes on their hard ridges. Shifting from foot to foot lowered her back pain but never more than a waving hand banished a mosquito. She studied the fat security man floating alone in his mental world. Her gaze slipped quickly past him to the lot, searching for a low, fast-moving form.

For the video, management was going to send not just filmmakers but a hair and makeup team.

"Panzón is going to get a modeling contract," joked Lourdes. "Then they'll make you manager—if they can fix that hair."

With warm fingers, she caught tufts of Sheila's brown hair and tugged them up and down experimentally.

As Sheila walked home, she found herself smiling.

"Suck me, baby!" roared a voice from a car.

A cool wind dissolved the blast of its motor and sent beech leaves scudding over the sidewalk. Sheila rubbed a hand over her scant hair, glad it wasn't long enough to flop in her face. Could the YourFood stylists make her look like a manager? Any day now, Jeff would be promoted. Running the store hadn't occurred to her, but now, with the map in her head, she wanted to protect its aisles.

"Raaaaah."

A faint rasp, barely a breath, rose from the packed ground beside her porch. There crouched Harapos, skinny and tense, her black tail twitching over her ridged back. She opened her mouth wide enough to yowl the scaly paint off the steps. Only a soft rush emerged.

"Catty, catty vroosh, goosh, goosh," whispered Sheila.

Harapos huffed out an answer. Sheila turned her locks, holding tight to her keys. The cat wove figure eights around her legs and butted her shins with its black-and-white head.

"Wait," she said, shaking a leg free. "First we straighten up; then comes dinner."

Harapos couldn't have eaten much dinner in the weeks she had lurked nearby. Her twisting revealed ribs under dull fur. Mad hunger was driving her in circles. Sheila ripped the roof off a can of sardines so that it curled into a menacing blade. She dug out a fish and dropped it with a plop. Harapos fell on it, crunching its threadlike bones. Sheila arranged a circle of crackers and topped each one with an oily gray chunk. Harapos butted her legs and rasped demands for more.

"Wait, cat," said Sheila.

She set the can on the floor, and with frantic licks, Harapos drove it into a corner. Sheila poured a glass of milk, turned on the TV, and put her fishy ring on the coffee table.

On *Big*, the determined doctor was berating an enormous woman. "That's what you *say* you're eating, but that's just your fantasy."

Sheila popped a salty fish cracker into her mouth. Harapos jumped onto the table and snatched a sardine.

"No!" Sheila leaped up, holding a pillow like a knight's

shield. "That's my fish! I'll give you yours. You touch that fish again, I'll kick you across the room!"

She didn't recognize her deep voice, but Harapos seemed to know its dark tones. The cat crouched, tense, ready to flee, studying Sheila with golden eyes.

EVERY HAIR

The cosmographer was gazing to the side, his fingers gripping a red wood table. White wisps of hair curled around his black hat like leaves stealthily seeking light. The white frill of his shirt must have tickled his neck, but his lips stayed pressed in a tight line. A black cloak warmed him as he sat still. Only the hairs on his collar were moving.

From his neck to his waist hung a horseshoe of fur in delicate tan and white. Soft and light, its hairs danced in a draft playing over his chest. Some animal must have grown those hairs once, some ermine that wriggled no more. On the old man, they came alive again, waving to anyone who cared to see.

No one stopped to look at the cosmographer. No wonder, since he never looked back. In room 16, the black-eyed Velázquez lady gazed sideways too, but her eyes stayed with you until, when you sat on the toilet, you felt her judging your private parts. The cosmographer seemed to be reminiscing as he posed, none too patiently. In the weeks it had taken to paint his portrait, his gray eyes had despaired of finding secrets in the surrounding room.

The painter had given him no background, no blue mountain with a spiraling path. Behind him hung only a moss-green scrim that darkened around his shoulders. With tiny strokes, the artist had rendered the white stubble of his chin and the silk loops fastening his shirt. In the fur collar, the painter had found his inspiration, a joy arcing between hand and eye. As the cosmographer sat imagining distant lands, the artist had painted every hair.

Two pairs of footsteps approached from room 5, where Dürer's browns warmed the dull walls. Between thunks of thick heels, a male voice floated like smoke.

"I think he's in here."

A tall, brown-haired boy steered a girl in black leggings, his hand poised on her slim shoulder. People used to dress up to go to museums. These two, like most young ones these days, appeared in pajamas and tights. Flesh bulged around a triangle of panties the black-haired girl groped to adjust.

"Look at him!"

The boy pushed her past the cosmographer, and she raised her eyes from her phone. He had brought her to Emperor Charles V, portrayed by the artist who'd painted the explorer. With his hanging jaw and red open mouth, Charles attracted most people in room 4.

"In the 1500s, this guy ruled most of Europe. And he was an idiot."

The girl shifted a pink knitted cap pulling at her long black hair. "Maybe he acted dumb to throw people off—so he could do what he wanted."

The boy scanned Charles's pale face for signs of deceit. "Why would people let you do what you want if they think you're dumb?"

"If they underestimate you, they don't watch you as much."

The girl's eyes moved to the blond knight across the room. After Charles, the knight in silver armor drew the most attention in room 4. The carved metal forced him

LAURA OTIS   •

into a wasp's shape, but his face, crowned by tight ringlets, looked pleased. With a soft sky above him and a misty village beyond, he looked out with a fresh, frank stare. The girl slipped from the boy's grip and aimed her phone. He followed her, pointing to the knight's ax.

"God, they used to decorate everything. That must have taken months to carve."

"To hack people up. Could have saved themselves trouble."

The girl's heels thunked off toward the mischievous Cranach girls in room 3.

Charles and the knight had backgrounds, and people approached to watch carts creep up winding roads. The sky overhead offered light denied the cosmographer by his moss-green scrim. The few people who walked through room 4 moved like moths toward the brighter paintings.

"Why do they even need you in there?" Olaf had asked Herwarth once.

Olaf, who guarded the Botticellis in room 50, had naughty blue eyes and a belly that flowed like a mudslide. Herwarth would have needed hours to answer Olaf's question. Just as Manfred had always said, Herwarth was too slow.

For Herwarth's eighth birthday, his parents had given him a box of sixty-four different-colored crayons. When he pulled back the lid, four rows of sixteen bright sticks stood like soldiers with waxy cone heads and tight wrappings. The army came organized according to shade, and Herwarth learned their formation. Each color had a name as luring as its shiny, tapered head. Midnight Blue, which looked like a bruise, taunted him with its blue-black voice. Spring Green sang high, out of tune, while Periwinkle hummed in its purple world. Burnt Sienna, which looked like Jan's dog's diarrhea, surprised him with its warm, cheerful sounds. From the moment Herwarth met the sixty-four colors, he looked for them everywhere, and he caught his breath when midnight blue flashed on a magpie's wing. In his head, he formed a pirate's treasure map showing where he could find each color.

With Jan, who lived in the house next door, Herwarth spent hours drawing. A thin, quiet boy with slick brown hair, Jan would breathe as his hand moved. A strange squiggle broke the line of his lips, a rope pulling the upper one toward his nose. As Jan drew, he licked his scar in quick flicks. He asked softly for colors, and when Herwarth handed him Forest Green, Jan's fingers felt dry and warm.

One day, when they were coloring at Herwarth's house, Herwarth said, "Let's have a contest!"

Jan stiffened but nodded silently.

"Let's each draw a house," said Herwarth, "the best house we can, and whoever draws the best house keeps the crayons tonight."

"Are you sure?" asked Jan. His thin face was tense.

Herwarth pushed a sheet of paper toward him and smiled. He closed his eyes until his own house shimmered before him. In the rain, its orange tile roof shone slick over its shuttered brown windows and chocolate door. Herwarth gripped Mahogany and tried to breathe as Jan did—one long, controlled stream for each line. His hand didn't quiver, and he looked with pride as the sides of his house emerged. Jan sat frowning and licking his scar as his hand wavered, as if he were unsure.

Herwarth reached for Sienna Brown, which he had heard was the color of roofs. Now that he'd laid the lines in three breaths, he would try to draw the tiles. Sienna Brown's long head had gone flat, and he had to tilt the crayon to outline each slate. With Forest Green, he formed the curves of bushes his house didn't have but should. By the door, he drew a white dog with black spots, the dog he had always wanted.

"Done!" he cried.

Jan looked up, startled, his hand still wavering.

"What have you got?" asked Herwarth.

Jan laid down Slate Gray and raised his drawing. Herwarth's face turned hot. In Jan's hand hung a house so real Herwarth wanted to move in. In some places, the gray surface shone, and in others, shadows darkened the stucco walls. Behind the open windows, people seemed to be moving, even though they were standing still. Jan had even included his dog, Rudi, squirting a brown pool of diarrhea.

Each breath made Herwarth feel hotter, as though his insides were red coals. His own house sat like a box with sides less straight than he had thought. An orange fish-scale hat weighed down the walls, straining their supporting lines.

Herwarth grabbed the box of crayons and hurled it across the room. Tight-wrapped soldiers shot every which way. Jan leaped up and clutched his drawing as though trying to save it from a demon. He ran for the door and didn't stop to close it.

Herwarth's mother found him because of the draft, since his explosion had made so little sound. Her gray eyes scanned the dead soldiers lying under the fat flakes of his torn drawing.

"You should be ashamed of yourself," she said. "We give you a nice present, and this is how you treat it? If you can't take care of your things, you don't deserve them."

Herwarth crawled over the scratchy gray rug until he found every crayon. Luckily, he had memorized their pattern. He laid them all in one rainbow strip before sliding them back into their box. Spring Green and Periwinkle had broken, but he pressed their halves together. In formation, their heads leaned only a little to one side. Flat-headed Sienna Brown and Slate Gray had survived, the colors he and Jan had used most.

Herwarth's mother sent him to Jan's house to apologize, but Jan wouldn't come to the door. Herwarth gave the green-and-yellow box to Jan's mother.

"They're all here," he said. "They're all in their right places. Some of them are broken. I'm sorry."

That night, Herwarth's father knocked on the door of his room, where his mother had sent him, as usual. Herwarth was supposed to think about what he had done and why he had been so bad. His father worked as an accountant, managing money people didn't deserve. If he came home and found trouble, he lashed out, and his hands could leave big blue spots. Herwarth's father folded his thick arms over his belly and breathed out in a long sigh. Light from the ceiling lamp gleamed on his bald head. From where Herwarth lay with smeared eyes, the light formed rainbow daggers pointing toward his father's glasses.

"So you fought with your friend and threw your new crayons all over the room?" he asked tiredly.

"I picked them up." Herwarth's voice sounded too high. "We didn't fight—he ran away."

His father's voice tightened. "You wouldn't have had to pick them up, and he wouldn't have run, if you hadn't behaved like a fool." His father gazed at him without moving.

"His drawing was so much better than mine." A sob broke Herwarth's voice. "It looked like a real house. It made me feel like nothing."

His father flexed his arms and stepped toward the bed. A tear rolling across Herwarth's cheek tried to hide in his ear.

"When somebody does something better than you, it makes you feel like nothing?"

Herwarth nodded. His father pulled off his glasses and rubbed his nose. This time, a rainbow ray pricked his lenses.

"Would you want to live in a world where no one did anything better than you? Go to the art museum and see those leaning shanties you draw? Go to the opera and hear that croaking you call singing? Buildings falling, bridges buckling, if people could even build them. But you would feel good because no one would be doing anything better than you. Is that the world you want to live in?"

Herwarth shook his head. More tears slid into his ears and tickled.

"The goddamn Nazis thought like that," said his father. "Look where it got us. You find something you're decent at, and do it. It sure as hell isn't drawing."

What did Herwarth do decently? Everything and nothing. His grades kept to the middle of the road like a car crossing an alligator-filled swamp. His father frowned at his report cards and nodded, as though they matched a spreadsheet in his head. Herwarth wondered what his father would do if he ever earned a perfect grade in anything.

Herwarth's reasonable success in math pointed toward ways he could earn his keep. Numbers comforted him with their dullness, like rubbing his head when he felt sad. But could he live with numbers forever? Numbers had nothing to say. Spending his life reckoning would mean living in a zombie world, floating in fluid silence.

Foreign languages irked him for the opposite reason: they made unnecessary noise. How could people have agreed to one metric system, one longitudinal grid, and then waste their lives learning each other's languages? Why not pick one and have everyone learn it? English would do. English words felt mushy in Herwarth's mouth, but they slid obligingly into place.

History, religion, geography, politics—you had to learn those to orient yourself. But once in place, they raised no more interest than marks on a measuring tape. Herwarth pitied people who liked philosophy, spending their lives on matters meant for momentary dreams. If anyone had asked Herwarth what he liked, he would have been afraid to say.

Herwarth loved the voices of colors. With a glance, he could hear colors murmuring as they approved of their neighbors or complained of contrasts. Where color met color, the whole universe began to speak. Herwarth loved art that brought forms to life by pitting one shade against another.

Music revealed another realm of voices, since tones spoke to Herwarth too. The major fourth of a police siren stabbed his ears; the minor third of a cuckoo fell like a cool drop. G resonated in forest green and spoke in an earnest, hoarse voice. Paired with brown D, which made a sturdy trunk, G formed a tree with a world of branches.

Herwarth studied piano with Frau Evertz, who respected his determined practicing. For hours each day, he groped for notes his stiff hands fought to find. When a clumsy slip turned a chord to a splat, Herwarth would cry with shame. After months of effort, he could play Schumann's green "Of Foreign Lands and Peoples" with only a few mistakes.

"Good, Herwarth," said Frau Evertz, "but could you make it more *musical*?"

Herwarth lowered his eyes. The desperate struggle to find the notes took all the strength of his hands and mind.

In art class, he felt freer to experiment, since his errors reached only his ears. He created cats with spiraling curves and dogs with leaning lines. No matter how hard he concentrated, his paintings never resembled anything real. His classmates scoffed.

"Art isn't photography," said their teacher, Herr Duncker. "If you just copy what's there, you've failed."

"But didn't Picasso learn to paint realistically *before* he found his own way?" asked a girl whose cats looked sleek enough to stroke.

Each day after classes ended, Herwarth painted or played on his keyboard. His mother liked to hear music in the house, but she complained if a fleck of color broke the bathroom sink's creamy white silence. Since Herwarth couldn't render forms, he experimented with shades. He studied how yellows whined next to browns and bickered with glowing blues. With his color chords, he created new forms: bright images with uncanny sounds. His quilt blocks of ochre, lemon, and teal just hadn't occurred yet in nature. Counselors advised against applying to art school.

"No prospects—stick with computers," they said. "Learn to do what the world needs, and paint on your own time. We'd all like to live from our art."

Herwarth's parents approved his choice of informatics, a field whose paths led to fertile lands. Unlike silent numbers, logic felt friendly, a companion with whom he could solve problems. Herwarth qualified for a study slot in Linberg, one of Germany's top programs. At first, his father balked at the distance. Silicon worked the same way in each town. Why not somewhere closer to home? But in Herwarth's mind, he had made the move. The blasted, resurrected city would welcome his color chords.

Linberg rose around Herwarth like a field planted with a million seeds. No one had bothered to bomb his trim town, but in Linberg, more than sixty years since the pounding, glass boxes flanked ornate facades, and crows cawed in muddy lots between government buildings. New forms were rising in the gaps, defiant as brazen weeds. Herwarth found an apartment in a flourishing district of loud-voiced Africans. On either side of his entrance, bright chords of red, yellow, and green marked a beauty shop and a convenience store. In Herwarth's one-room apartment, he placed his easel near the window, so he could watch the boisterous encounters below. After paying his rent, he spent the rest of his father's check on a yearly museum ticket and went to an art museum each day.

Informatics kept him studying in fear, like a metal woman set to spurn him. The other students gripping her cold skirt seemed to feel no urge for friendship. Herwarth found companions in a men's chorus, whose singers welcomed his shaky bass. When he could, he left his computer to explore Linberg's thriving neighborhoods. In the poorest districts, some dull buildings still bore the pockmarks of Allied shells. In the richest ones, dogs wore thicker, brighter sweaters than most of the children where Herwarth lived.

He paused near a teeming construction site, thinking about what the world wanted. At home, he had had tasks to perform and had done them. No one had ever asked Herwarth what he wanted to do. At his feet, a dog strained to squeeze out a turd, and a pale man shivered while he waited. In a Turkish snack bar, a thick-armed man shaved meat from a turning spit. Would it hurt the world so badly if Herwarth did what he craved? Who could know that no one would ever value his color chords? How good could someone's work be if it were driven only by fear? On a November day of chilling rain, he quit the informatics program.

Disgusted, his father withdrew all support, and Herwarth had to find work fast. His friends in the choir suggested restaurants, boutiques.

"You look so good," said a pudgy tenor. "Slim, straight. That intense look? You'd pull people into a shop."

The warm singer might have been right, since within a week, Herwarth received offers. But another branch of work drew him. At the art museums, he had seen signs saying that the State Museums wanted security guards. The work would pay eight euros an hour, and the singers advised against it. As a janitor, Herwarth could earn more. But he already saw himself in the Fine Arts Museum, helping people find their favorite paintings. He could spend his days in that hushed space, savoring his own thoughts. At night, he could paint, sing, and play; on weekends, he could walk the untamed neighborhoods. The men he met cringed when they heard of his job, but they distinguished his labor from his work. Herwarth was an artist, enduring boredom so he could eat. No one believed he liked being a guard.

As Herwarth surveyed his world in room 4, counting gave each day a unique shape. When he paced, twelve strides took him from the Cranach entrance to the cosmographer in the far corner. Nineteen paintings hung on the walls— eighteen if you counted the diptych as one. All had been created in Southern Germany between about 1450 and 1550. When he scanned the mosaic of postcards in the shop, he found that room 4 hadn't provided one tile. Not even pale Charles V appeared, with his coral-red mouth and jutting jaw. Herwarth couldn't remember the last time a visitor had crept close enough to spike an alarm. People set off sirens all the time in 28, the Vermeer room, where fools tried to follow the brushstrokes with their fingers. Today that irreverent boy and girl had nosed closer to Charles than anyone had in a long time.

A few years back, Olaf had challenged the guards to guess which painting was worth most. All twenty-five guards had to throw in ten euros, and the winner would take the pot. Olaf bet on a circular Botticelli where a wavy-haired woman swam among blissful boys. Olaf bragged that he fucked them on alternating nights, the wavery beauty and the angel boys too.

Ludmilla, who watched over the Velázquez lady, swore she would have brought the highest price. One night, after closing, a young actor who spoke good Spanish came to the Velázquez room to shoot a museum ad. Dark-eyed, with rich brown hair, he looked like the Velázquez woman's son. In the ad, he wore a guard's navy-blue suit and red tie, but no actual guard appeared on-screen. As the film rolled, he seduced a bright-eyed visitor by pronouncing names that rang like minor chords: Diego Rodríguez de Silva y Velázquez, Bartolomé Esteban Murillo, Francisco de Zurbarán. If you came to this museum, the ad implied, you might meet *him*. You could hang out with *them*.

When the ad played in theaters, Ludmilla swore she heard a blonde girl say, "No shit! He works as a guard here?"

The actor's ad pulled in visitors that the Fine Arts Museum sorely needed. Herwarth had heard rumors that the museum might close, and its highlights move to a context wing in the Modern Art Museum. Nowadays, few people wanted to see art created with painstakingly fine strokes.

In the contest, Ludmilla stood a good chance with Velázquez, as did Izzet with the Vermeer lady in her yellow coat. Gazing anxiously at a necklace in her extended hands, she seemed to wonder what its price might be. Ever since a brooding British actor had played Vermeer on-screen, room 28 hadn't known a quiet moment. All day long, Izzet had to keep people off the yellow lady, plus another in coral who was being pressed to drink a shimmering glass of wine.

Izzet had a good case with Vermeer, but Herwarth won the contest because he cheated. Well, not if you considered that he and Manfred were one person then, so that you couldn't say where Manfred's mind stopped and his began.

Herwarth set his stake on Caravaggio but won only fifty euros, since four of the twenty-five guards voted the same way. Herwarth might have voted for Caravaggio even if Manfred hadn't scanned the auction sites. The Italian's laughing Eros lured men and women alike. Its tiny dick exerted a magnetic pull like a node at the center of the universe.

With his winnings, Herwarth invited Manfred to dinner. On a glowing May evening in asparagus season, Manfred found the sweet, nubbed white stalks perfect.

"Good guess," he said, his black eyes warm with irony.

Olaf had dampened Herwarth's triumph by saying no one had backed a painting in room 4.

"No crook with half a brain would steal them," he said. "When they close this place, we'll have to call a junk dealer to haul them out."

"Some people like them," said Herwarth. "They're part of German history. No one's going to close us down."

Herwarth's job at the museum felt safe, but he wished that in this vault of beauty, he could be of greater use. He could answer people's questions.

"Where's the bathroom?"

"Where am I?"

"How do I get to the Vermeer room?"

He could warn visitors when they came too close to a painting, jostled each other, or talked too loudly. Ludmilla had once ejected three teenagers for laughing, and their boss, the Dark Knight, had backed her. It pleased Herwarth that the slim, black-haired head of security respected the museum's sacred hush.

At least in room 4, you could see real paintings with people and mountains and towns. Olaf's friend Lars at the Contemporary Art Museum said that there, they had it rough. In a room big enough for a hundred dancers, someone had hung half-built black cabinets on the white walls. Any carpenter would have taken one look and hammered them apart for scrap. For three months, Lars had to guard this art, which came with an explanatory brochure. In ninety days, not one person had shown interest. Some glanced at the cubbies out of cultural duty, but most moved straight to the window. The bicyclists gliding down the glistening street brought light to people's eyes. Thank God the cabinets were just visiting, said Lars. If he'd had to watch those black cubbies one more day, he would have hammered them to death himself.

Apart from Herwarth, few of the guards seemed to hold much stake in the art that defined their worlds. Manfred would have cringed at the sight of Olaf, whose jacket couldn't cover his bulging belly. The guards wore their blue suits badly, their red ties askew over marshmallow guts. Mohammed, already fat at thirty, shrugged his coat off his shoulders until it gripped him like a straitjacket. Degenerates, Manfred would have said, unworthy of having human forms. Stuffing themselves full of sausage and chips until they looked like the trash bags they were.

Manfred liked the way Herwarth stood. He had an

arresting profile. Manfred spotted him at an intermission in the Concert Hall refreshment room. Manfred watched him all through the Ninth Symphony—each time Manfred told the story, it changed a shade. Herwarth winced at the crashing chords as though he were struck by an angry hand. He leaned into the running melodies as though watching a black dog race through purple crocuses. He rejoiced, and he recoiled, but his features stayed set. To Manfred, he looked as complex as Beethoven, as intense as his raging music.

Manfred touched Herwarth's arm as they descended the Concert Hall steps. In the frigid night, the new moon looked sharp enough to cut. On either side, church domes glowed in massive cylinders of light.

"Are you all right?" asked the man who had touched Herwarth. "I can see that you felt that music."

The man stood taller than Herwarth and fixed him with close-set dark eyes. His tastefully cut hair whitened toward the temples, and his long face had been shaved hours before. The crowd pushed them down into the plaza, where the man raised an arm, inviting Herwarth to step aside. Like Moses, thought Herwarth. As though he ruled that shining stone sea.

"My name is Manfred," he said in a soft bass. "I noticed you—living that music. I'd like to know you. Will you have coffee with me?"

Herwarth trembled as he nodded. In his charcoal coat, Manfred moved with the grace of an aging cat. He led Herwarth to a café and laughed at his order: a round container of Bircher muesli and a white mug of peppermint tea. Manfred asked for an espresso, which his fine lips seemed to kiss.

"Won't that keep you up?" asked Herwarth.

Manfred met his eyes and smiled. The white cup lingered against his lip. "Nothing stops my sleep," he said. "That's a train you can't derail."

Herwarth had never followed a man home after meeting him hours before. Usually, after some uneasy meals, men entered him as though doing him a favor, then ignored or threatened him when he called. But Manfred marveled at Herwarth's painting, his music, his work as a museum guard. As Herwarth spoke of Velázquez and Vermeer, Manfred's dark eyes glowed with amusement. They lost their irony only when Herwarth spoke of colors, in a voice he hadn't known he had.

"Yes," said Manfred. "We don't need to worship God—some ridiculous human projection. But colors, sounds—they deserve our respect. You respect things. You respect life."

Manfred's eyes reddened, and he lowered his gaze. Herwarth grasped Manfred's hand. For a moment, they sat, joined only by a tremble that settled to serene stillness.

In the night, Herwarth counted Manfred's breaths as he listened to eerie chimes. Three ceramic plates—from the sound, it was three—rocked against the balcony wall in gusts of wind. With scraping rings, the plates sang out discordantly. Were they going to fall? Manfred might have known if he were awake, but he had slipped into sleep as soon as they slid apart. Herwarth touched Manfred's warm thigh, but he didn't stir. Outside, the plates rang in the wind. They chimed what might have been a cry for help or a song of reckless delight.

Manfred insisted on seeing Herwarth's art. At first, Herwarth balked. Since he had moved to Linberg, few had entered his apartment, and no one had seen his paintings. But from the moment Manfred touched Herwarth, every door to his being opened. His breath quickened as Manfred glanced at the Ghanaian beauty shop and grocery. In the stairwell, Manfred's eyes caught gouges on the walls, but his steps didn't break rhythm. Herwarth led him to his easel, where, on a canvas, brown was growling at red. Manfred picked up the painting and tilted it to catch different intensities of light. A cry rang out from the street below, where one boy was kicking another.

"How long have you been painting these?" asked Manfred.

He set down the painting, and Herwarth realized he'd been holding his breath. The orange red jeered back at the brown.

"Since high school," said Herwarth.

Manfred's eyes swept the compact kitchen, the silver keyboard, the single bed. "You don't hang them up," he said. "This one's good. Why don't you put them on your walls? Where do you keep them?"

"I—I rent a storage unit." Heat rose to Herwarth's face.

"And you've never tried to show them? Sell them?"

"No," murmured Herwarth. "I didn't think—I wouldn't know …"

Manfred frowned at the painting. "Well! I like this one. I can hear it—the red chiding the brown. Like a married couple. The red makes more noise, but the brown is holding its own."

Herwarth gave Manfred the red-and-brown painting, and Manfred hung it in his hall. He didn't return to Herwarth's studio, but he welcomed him to his own apartment with carved ceilings, broad bookshelves, and a grand piano. Manfred made Herwarth open his storage unit, and he surveyed every color chord. Manfred asked him their names, but Herwarth couldn't answer. It hadn't occurred to him to name them.

Manfred called art galleries; he called his friends. A few of the paintings sold. But the galleries weren't interested, and Herwarth suspected Manfred's friends bought the color chords to please him. As they inspected the paintings, they assessed Manfred with sideways glances.

"At least you try," said Manfred. "At least you paint. You sing. You play. A failed artist isn't one who can't sell his work. It's one who doesn't paint."

When Manfred's architectural designs involved color, he consulted Herwarth and often took his advice. "My undiscovered genius," he called him. At one dinner party, he introduced Herwarth to his friends as the "guardian of art."

From the men's laughter, Herwarth knew he was ludicrous, a thing that shouldn't *be*. But through Manfred, his sense of color was shaping people's homes. If Manfred didn't respect him, he wouldn't ask his opinion.

Herwarth cooked, ate, and slept in Manfred's space, but Manfred urged him to keep his walk-up studio.

"It's good to have someplace apart," he said. "I can draw at work, but you can't paint in that museum."

Herwarth liked redefining his space as a studio, and as his locks clicked open, one-two-three, he released breath he hadn't known he'd held. He began painting a new series of browns—browns cringing against sulfurous yellows, browns baffled by boisterous purples. He didn't tell Manfred about his new paintings, and after that first inventory, Manfred didn't ask. He seemed to value the fact of Herwarth's painting more than the work itself. It pleased Herwarth to be painting in secret, making movements Manfred couldn't see. Manfred might have liked the way Herwarth stood, but he didn't like the way he moved.

Herwarth hadn't realized that he was slow or that he was always seeking something. At the farmers market, when he dug in his pack, he would rise to find Manfred smirking.

"Why can't you keep your phone in your pocket?" Manfred asked. "When you bend over with your rump in the air like that, you look like a female sheep waiting to be serviced."

Herwarth laughed along with a slim couple squeezing by, but his stomach clenched. He couldn't leave an expensive device in his pocket, begging to be freed by a thief's hand. At the bottom of his pack, in a Ziploc bag, his phone lay sealed and safe. His phone shared the space with his wallet, his glasses, his rain gear, black-bread sandwiches, and plastic bags. In his pack, he carried all he needed to survive in a battering city. His phone just had a devilish way of hiding in his waterproof jacket.

When Herwarth joined Manfred in his travels, he did his best to move gracefully. He imagined a camera filming them in a pan shot as they crossed Charles de Gaulle Airport. Together, they should have advanced like twin dancers, not like Nureyev walking his pet bear. Fear gripped Herwarth, tightening every move. Manfred never seemed to think about his own movements.

Despite Manfred's chiding, he wanted Herwarth close. He invited him on business trips, even when all they could do together was sleep. He acknowledged Herwarth's skill with a tiny nod when Herwarth named the key of music flowing from the radio. After taking his pleasure with Herwarth in the dark, Manfred would ask, "How did you get to *be* like this?" In daylight, Manfred's question resonated with a different tone.

Herwarth struggled to talk with Manfred's friends, whose quick thoughts darted like bats. He had always found it hard to converse, since people didn't perceive sounds or colors as he did, and their thoughts made little sense. He noticed that Manfred kept him away from most clients, inviting him only where he could do the least harm.

Manfred did ask Herwarth to dinner with an American whose Linberg apartment he was redesigning.

"I'm thinking cool tones," said the twitchy man, "to go with this gorgeous, delicate northern light." He glanced from Manfred to Herwarth, on whom his eyes lingered.

"Right," said Manfred. "You'll want to keep those 1909 windows. Celebrate the natural light."

The man laid down his fork and smiled. "I love Nordic! Blues, whites, browns—"

"Not blue and brown!" exclaimed Herwarth.

A small piece of shrimp flew from his mouth and stuck to the enraptured man's chin. Herwarth swallowed as fast as he could. Eating and talking were a deadly mix.

"Blue with brown—that could be a tritone," warned Herwarth. "They could fight, and the blue could kill the brown."

The man passed his napkin over his chin and glanced at Manfred. His voice emerged lower, tighter. "I didn't know you had a synesthete on your payroll."

"Not exactly." Manfred looked at Herwarth with long-suffering irony. "Herwarth is my hobby."

Herwarth said little else through the meal, and Manfred and the American endured him like the ghost of an ill-chosen ex-wife. Herwarth's stomach stayed tight on the tram ride home, but Manfred took his hand and pressed it. In the night, Manfred made love to him with slamming blows.

"God, I love fucking you," he whispered. And he fell asleep.

At breakfast, Manfred asked Herwarth to leave.

"This would work if it were just the two of us," he said. "Go to bed, and talk about art. But I can't live with you. I don't see how anyone could. You don't know how to live in this world."

"There isn't just one way to live!" Herwarth's voice collapsed as the tears came. "I live fine! I was doing fine before I met you."

"Fine?" Manfred unleashed his disgust. "With your talent, earning minimum wage? Living alone in a ghetto? Do you even know anyone besides me?"

Herwarth stood. His chair slid back with a hideous scrape. "You wanted to know me," he said. "I didn't ask to know you. You're the one with the void. All the men in the world couldn't fill your gaps."

Herwarth still had his job, his apartment. Some men tossed by rich lovers found themselves on the street. He had merely fallen back to his starting square, as in that Chutes and Ladders game he used to hate. It relieved him that Manfred hadn't visited him at work and that he'd said nothing of Olaf or Ludmilla. Manfred hadn't permeated all of him, and he found unpoisoned ground on which to grow. With relief, he went back to his browns and the vibrant paintings of room 4.

Each day, the cosmographer's expression changed, as though registering new thoughts. Without breaking their sideward gaze, his eyes sometimes brightened; other days, they faded with boredom. His lips stayed set in a tight line, but in moments, the line broke. Sitting for that portrait must have tortured him. When he dreamed, his fingers relaxed on the red board; other days, he gripped the wood for dear life. Grimly enduring when Herwarth left him Tuesday night, he might be savoring a secret joke on Wednesday. Anytime Herwarth looked at the cosmographer, his mind seemed to have shifted, as though his thoughts were moving as he sat.

Herwarth had thought a cosmographer studied stars, but he learned that he explored the world. A cosmographer traveled and wrote down what he saw.

Imagine earning a living doing that!

No wonder sitting still was maddening him. He had died the year the portrait was made. Maybe he'd known how little time he had left to cross mountains whose stony trails called.

And the painter had held him there, pinned like a beetle on a board.

"One more day," the artist must have begged.

One more day to paint each hair on the ruff of a man raging to be gone. A cosmographer who must have wished the painter's brushes would blaze like torches in hell. To create this picture, an aging man had given his last weeks, and an artist, his greatest skill. Not even Velázquez could paint a face that changed each day like the Ionian Sea under Herwarth and Manfred's window.

That trip to Taormina had been their last, now almost a year ago. Herwarth always woke early, and he loved to watch the newborn light on Manfred's face as his last dream flowered. The sun that turned the sea from purple to blue found beauty in Manfred's stillness. Asleep, he didn't taunt Herwarth for counting the 665 steps down to the beach. He didn't exhale with disgust when Herwarth groped in his pack. The morning light showed only the goodness in Manfred's love of grace.

The cosmographer looked sad but curious that day, his right eyebrow raised, his hazel eyes keen. Thick-heeled boots approached from the Dürer room with a slow, measured beat. A slim, black-haired woman entered without pausing to take her bearings. Breasts barely stretched her ribbed yellow sweater, which sang like forsythia in April. As she walked, a navy-blue skirt with white stars rippled against her black tights. It had been weeks since a woman in a skirt entered room 4. Nowadays, women regarded skirts as the accoutrements of slaves or fools. They seemed to have forgotten that flowing cloth lured the mind like ocean waves.

With her determined step, this woman didn't move like someone trying to attract. Only a few black wisps hung from her clipped-up hair, and her brown eyes soon found their target. With even paces, she crossed to the knight and offered him her gaze. Under his blond curls, his pale eyes looked out at her expectantly. His fingers tightened around his ax. Her breathing slowed to a sleeper's pace until they stood as one in stillness. Only when her movements ceased did Herwarth recognize the girl in black leggings.

Without her boyfriend's steering hand, she inhabited herself differently.

Couldn't she feel the cosmographer's eyes? The old man had shifted his gaze. The yellow lines of her shirt, which merged at the waist, excited him like veins of gold in mountain rock. If only she would turn to see the finest creation of a painter's life. Herwarth had only to say a word. What part of the knight painting drew her? He stepped closer to look. Her dark eyes stayed fixed on the man's, with only occasional flits up the hill.

"There's a nice painting over here."

The woman started as Herwarth's voice flowed. With trembling fingers, she tucked some black hair behind her ear.

"Right over here—just behind you."

The woman folded her thin arms and compressed her lips like the cosmographer. She smiled coolly and followed Herwarth across the room.

"Look!" His voice rushed, uncontrolled. He pointed to the fur collar, his finger rising as close as it dared. "Isn't this amazing? Think how much work—how much time—it took to paint. All those years of learning."

The woman's small dark eyes glanced at the fur and rose quickly to the explorer's.

"He looks angry," she murmured. "You can see his feelings. That's where the real work went in."

Sure enough, the cosmographer looked grim. His lips had thinned, and his grip on the table tightened. He didn't glance at the young woman reading him, but Herwarth sensed he was following each breath.

"No one looks." Herwarth's voice wavered. "And it's a brilliant painting—brilliant. I can tell you like art. I just wanted you to see it."

The black-haired woman turned to face him. She was taller than he'd realized, and her close-set brown eyes easily met his.

"Thank you," she said flatly. "I can see why you like it. Thanks for making me look."

Her wedge heels thunked back toward the Dürers with a quicker rhythm than before.

The next day, Herwarth took to pacing room 4. For weeks, he trod the space like a panther at the zoo. The old man never shifted his gaze, but Herwarth sensed his urge to walk. Even exploring a ship-sized room would have been preferable to that eternal sitting.

Heavy steps crossed the Cranach room faster than most visitors cared to move. Herwarth turned to find Olaf framed in the door, his belly sliding into room 4.

"Dark Knight wants to see you," he said.

The guards used this term for Gisela Ritter, the slim, black-haired head of security. Frau Ritter liked Olaf and spent hours grating him with her raspy voice. Herwarth looked dubiously at Olaf, whose blue eyes shone with amusement.

"She said now. I asked Mohammed to look in." Olaf's

eyes circled the empty room. "Go on. Nobody's going to grope your paintings."

With strides the cosmographer would have envied, Herwarth paced toward Frau Ritter's office. What had he done? He could think of no offense. Did she want him to change shifts, watch a different room? Frau Ritter's office lay at the museum's apex, where the Italian, French, and Spanish wing merged with the German, Flemish, and Dutch. Drawing tight breaths, Herwarth journeyed through time, admiring Dutch skaters, shuddering at fleshy women. He startled Izzet, who was watching a young man's fingers dance inches from Vermeer's coral lady. Herwarth pointed toward Frau Ritter's office, and Izzet returned his attention to the eager boy.

Herwarth's knock hit the door with a broken rhythm Frau Ritter seemed to recognize.

"Herwarth? Come in," she called, and he passed into a dim, cramped space.

Frau Ritter motioned for him to sit down as though easing an imaginary foot into a shoe. Her black hair had thinned, and her high cheekbones made her look gaunt. She might have been older than the guards had guessed, or maybe smoking was doing her in. Frau Ritter looked at Herwarth with stern dark eyes.

"Herwarth, we've had another complaint."

He rubbed his damp hands against his thighs. "A complaint?"

Frau Ritter brought her fingers to her palm in quick succession, one-two-three-four-five.

"Yes." She cleared her throat. "Another woman. She said you approached her and ordered her to look at a painting. Lecturing, patronizing, as if she were a child."

"No!" he gasped.

Frau Ritter kept playing her unseen castanet.

"I do remember a woman," he said slowly, "a few weeks ago. I asked her to look at a painting. But it was a suggestion, not an order."

Frau Ritter twisted her dry lips to the side. She raised a paper and shook it until it rippled.

"She filed a formal complaint. With the State Museums of the German Ministry of Culture. She said you were being disrespectful."

"No! I would never disrespect anyone!"

Every atom of Frau Ritter intensified. "How would you define your job here?" she asked.

On Frau Ritter's top shelf, a Botticelli beauty gazed sadly down from a postcard.

"To—to protect great art," he said. "And help people see it."

Frau Ritter shook her head. A few black wisps wavered.

"No." Her voice could have filed a nail. "You're here to protect art and assist patrons—*if* they ask for information, *if* they want to hear from you. You do not approach people. You do not disrupt their thoughts. They're communing with some of the best art in the world. If you violate that, you disrespect them."

"But what's the point?" Herwarth's voice sharpened.

"Stand there silent all day while people walk by and don't see? Those artists—they put their whole lives into these paintings. All their wisdom, their passion. They didn't do that to be ignored."

Frau Ritter gazed at a point over his head. "That is not your problem, Herwarth. If you want to teach art, earn a degree. You're denying patrons the right to decide which art they want to see."

Herwarth met Frau Ritter's eyes, one of whose lids was sagging. "That painting I showed her—the cosmographer—it's brilliant," he said. "The detail. The personality. Four hundred and fifty years old, and he looks alive. That artist was a genius. He gave everything he had. And the old man had to sit there for weeks! People just walk by him. He deserves better than that."

Frau Ritter's frown sharpened. "Herwarth, why women?"

Herwarth's breath stopped in midflow. "Women?" he asked.

One glance sufficed for most women to know he was inert. Female visitors paid no more heed to him than to the mousetrap in the corner. Frau Ritter patted the letter, which she had laid on her desk.

"We've had two complaints about you now, both from women. I know you're not sexually harassing them." Her lips twitched, but she quashed her thought.

"No! Never!"

"You've worked here longer than anyone. You're the most reliable, the most punctual, the best dressed."

Again, she stopped, in deference to a rule as strict as the ban against approaching patrons.

"If someone told me one of the others was harassing women, I might believe it." She smiled as she ducked into a thought. "But no one's had a problem with anyone but you. What is it with you and women? Why are you telling women to look at your favorite painting, but not men?"

"I—because they listen to me. Because they look at me," he said. "When they see the painting, they seem to like it. That woman thanked me. She thanked me!"

"That's a rapist's logic," said Frau Ritter.

Herwarth trembled, and his eyes turned hot.

"You're forcing yourself on people." Frau Ritter seemed to find her voice as Herwarth lost his. "On women, because you think they'll be more amenable. And you're claiming they like it."

"No, it's not like that!" he cried. "I care about the art— the artist."

"You should care about people." Her voice grated the air. "The women into whose thoughts you're inserting yourself."

Frau Ritter's eyes reddened, and Herwarth wondered how deep her sense of violation ran.

"I'm sorry," he murmured. "I won't do it again. You don't have to worry."

"Oh, I'm not worried." Frau Ritter seemed to have banished her ghost. "I'm telling you. If this happens again, your work here is done. Respect the patrons—or you're gone. Do you understand?"

Herwarth nodded.

In the next weeks, Herwarth kept a stranglehold on his urge to speak. The people drifting through room 4 stayed sealed in their thoughts, into which the cosmographer did not enter. Frau Ritter had been right. People had a right to contemplate unaccosted. Especially women, who might have been enjoying a few precious hours away from men's guiding hands. When no one asked the way to the bathrooms, Herwarth passed whole days without talking. He focused his mind on the sounds of feet: squeaky leather, sticky rubber, gouging heels. From the weak soup of sound in the Cranach room, he summoned pictures of fat men, tired tourists, angry girls. He guessed not just their appearances but how long it would take before they breached the portal of room 4.

On a day of pounding west wind, an odd mix of sound reached Herwarth's ears. Soft friction and a steady hum bathed a set of leather footsteps. Together, two male voices were weaving a fine, dark tapestry. The gentle blend lingered in the Cranach room, then approached at a measured pace. A motored wheelchair rolled into room 4, its rapt owner glancing sideways at Manfred.

In a year, Manfred hadn't thickened or thinned, though he seemed to have intensified. His charcoal pants and cloud-gray shirt fit him comfortably, but his well-timed movements had quickened. Manfred's dark eyes warmed slightly as they assessed Herwarth.

"So this is the room in need of protection?"

The slim, brown-haired man in the chair scanned the room in a steady curve. "I would protect it," he said. He smiled at Herwarth and revealed a chipped front tooth.

"Ah, Werner!" Manfred rolled his eyes. He rested his hands on a stuffed black pack hanging behind Werner's chair.

Werner's eyes unsettled Herwarth as they searched him from burning forehead to worn black shoes. His gaze seemed powered by a hundred stories, to whose images he was comparing Herwarth.

Manfred tried to push Werner's chair, but it would only move under its own power.

"Look—there's Charles V!" Manfred pointed across the room, where Charles's coral mouth glowed.

Herwarth turned his eyes to Werner's, in which a few flecks of green flashed.

"There's a great painting over here," said Herwarth. "Would you like to see it?" He raised a trembling hand toward the old man in fur.

"Sure."

Werner pressed a lever, and his chair hummed a fifth higher. He rolled toward the cosmographer, and Manfred and Herwarth followed with matched paces.

"Amazing," whispered Werner. "You can feel the stubble of his face. That shirt against his neck. I can feel what he's feeling." He kept his eyes on the cosmographer, who had frozen under his gaze.

"That fur," said Herwarth. "Think how long it must have taken."

"Yes." Werner's voice came like a choral response. "To paint like that, you'd have to believe every atom in the universe matters."

Manfred reached down to press Werner's hand. "Shall we go on?"

Werner studied the cosmographer's eyes and tried to follow his gaze. He glanced toward the Dürer door and sighed.

"Yes, let's keep going. I like your room, Herwarth."

Manfred stood in the Dürer door, a freeze-frame of impatient style. "Goodbye, Herwarth," he said. "I can see why you like it here."

Manfred ducked out of sight, and with a prolonged chord, Werner rolled after him. In the Dürer door, Werner paused to wave, his thin hand stirring the air. Herwarth couldn't tell whether the wave was meant for him or for the cosmographer. The old man exhaled, his breath unsettling his soft fur. Warm energy rose in the cosmographer, suffusing the room through his outward gaze.

ESCALATOR

I hate people who move in clumps, blocking the flow of life. The wider they are, the slower they walk, the likelier to glom together. Bulk always attracts more bulk, the way plaques choke blood to the heart. Fat couples roll along, arms linked, like lovestruck semis plugging Autobahn lanes. Families float in groups of five or six at paces set in their own heads. They cling together in dense bunches as though they'd cease to be if they lost their grip. Kids hinged to their mothers' arms swing out like gates, barring the way. They give no thought to any movement but their own, to people moving with a purpose.

Clutching her pen, June realized she was breathing as though dodging hulks on the sidewalk. She had conjured her obstructors so well that she was nearly panting. Didi had always known when she slipped into a horror fantasy, because her breathing changed. She stopped taking the air she needed and sipped it furtively, as though someone would whack her if he caught her breathing.

"Take deep breaths!" he had demanded.

Even as a memory, Didi's voice drilled through the din of Circle Center Mall. But Didi would command her breath no more. Didi was dead.

Months ago, he had come to Translate-OR with marketing copy from his cell phone company. To win customers whose German was dim, Deutschkom wanted to lure them in English. Birgit, June's boss, had put her in charge, though June usually worked in a back room. No one could match German with English as June's impulses led her to do. Clients beamed at sentences driven by energy they hadn't known their minds could wield. Each word had a life, a personality, and the words someone invited to his party (most clients were male) revealed his ethos like a roomful of bonding guests.

Birgit reported the clients' awe: "I didn't realize, but this is just what I wanted to say. You took a liberty—but I like this better than what I wrote."

Carolin, who ran reception, described the smiles of white-haired men in raincoats who picked up their translations personally.

June herself rarely evoked smiles from clients or from anyone she ever met. When people saw her, their shoulders tightened, and they frowned as though scanning a room tinged with mold.

"If this is a cruise ship, you're the engine," said Birgit. "Every day, I thank God you left the US to work here. Let Carolin handle entertainment. Concentrate on what you do best."

Looking down on a courtyard with blue, brown, and yellow dumpsters, June listened to words and imagined minds. She had met Didi because the wet day he walked in, Carolin's day care had to close early.

Thin and quick in his movements, Didi considered her with mocking blue eyes.

"Na?" he asked, a sound was so irreverent it sparked a smile. "What did you do with the woman who sits here?"

"Human sacrifice," said June.

"The gods didn't want you?" Didi's lip twitched.

"They want me to translate," said June. "What have you got for me?"

Birgit honored Didi's wishes when, for the first time, a client wanted to work with her top translator. In Didi's catlike head, words flowed through a *Wackelkontakt*, a link that transmitted unreliably. Language launched no cascades in his mind. Anchored to stone-block meanings, his words didn't commune. He seemed more interested in June's mental swirls: her aversion to family, her loss of a university job.

"Why build your life around relationships forced on you when you were helpless?" she asked. "Why live in a cell when you can walk around freely?"

Over pepper-and-mushroom pizza, Didi revealed that he had been walking on swampy ground for some time. His wife's love soaked him like fine rain when he craved the smash of a storm. But when he ran headfirst into hurricanes, they engulfed him, flooding any road out. Years ago, he'd had a hell of a time fleeing an American. She had cried at him well over a year, her tears aimed as though shot from a water gun. Why couldn't people enjoy each other without levying an emotional tax? June didn't seem born for drama. Fantasies wouldn't colonize her mind.

Sometimes June felt like a translation of Didi when he slammed into her to purge his *Frust*. Her fine legs doubled his on a smaller scale; only the entry between them made her different. She accepted Didi grudgingly because most men looked at her with unease. June hated rules, but his terms didn't anger her, since she felt no urge to grip him and cry.

When she'd last seen him a few weeks ago, his mouthed kiss from the doorway had seemed fond. But she wouldn't be meeting her German self again. Didi's death had come so strangely it had inspired legends online.

He had been rehearsing Mozart's "Ave Verum Corpus" with the choir where he had sung for years. With his chin on his fist, his eyes closed, he had listened while the sopranos sang. He'd been known to nap while others practiced, so no one had missed him until the men's turn. His neighbor had elbowed him, and he'd crumpled as though the stringy bass had shoved a sock monkey.

"A mystery death," sang one X post. "Shows how little scientists know."

Lean, athletic, Didi's body had stopped living. His life had ended for no reason.

Saturday morning, the choir would sing at his funeral, and June felt an irresistible pull. In his misty wife, what form would grief take? Would the water gun show, crying harder than ever? June doubted they knew about Didi's translator, and she longed to compare his women to their descriptions. She had come to Circle Center seeking black clothes but had ended up in the basement, writing.

Whoever had built Circle Center Mall had read Dante but not an efficiency manual. Shops rose from the depths in tight rings, connected by anxious escalators. To buy clothes, you had to reach the right ring and ride up fuming if your way was blocked. What most people wanted lay beneath: the supermarket, the food court, the restrooms. As though eating or peeing were a mortal sin but buying a black blouse, less so. Down below, June suspected her best bet for black would be H&M on level three. In an hour, the shops would be closing. She had sat writing for too long.

Turbulence rippled through the up escalator as two brown-haired girls fought their way down. Shifting bodies blocked the way up; June would have to grind along at the machine's pace. She took her place behind a Goth girl whose black hair trembled at its purple tips. On her oily head, a broad part revealed pale skin crusted with dandruff. The solid back inches from June's face turned her stomach tight. People's backs revealed their ugliness. And their swollen bottoms seemed to jeer, "I'm ahead of you. I'm better than you. Just so you know, here's my ass in your face." The heavy-set girl stood there inert, as though whatever she'd done to look dead white had drained away her strength.

Laughing, one of the adventurous girls pushed by. She had almost reached the bottom. A space opened, and June stepped up, but just as quickly, the running girl's sister shot down. Hardness slammed the front of June's body, and she grabbed for the rail. Instead of plastic, her fingers met round warmth, a soft and giving mound. June whipped back her hand as if she had stroked a snake.

"Excuse me," she gasped.

The giddy thirteen-year-old seemed not to care that a strange woman had cupped her breast. The scrumptiousness of that warmth frightened June. She had known so little touch in her life. Her parents hadn't hit, and they hadn't yelled, but they'd avoided contact as if she were poison ivy. Men had supplied touch in a form different from the spongy wonder she'd just felt.

Before the running girls accused her, she had to get out. They had reached the food court, and here she stood, trapped behind this dull Goth. Did the girls have a mother? Had cameras caught her inept grab? Was the exit on level one or level two? Were bearded security men awaiting her there? No one would believe she'd groped a girl by mistake.

Aging, childless women might break any rule. Detached from young and old bodies, they became suspect. God knew what they might do to please themselves if they didn't have to feed, wipe, or transport others. June pictured a crowd surging at the exit: crying girls, rabid mother, indignant police. A circle of shoppers would close around her, push her down, kick out their rage. Spitting, screaming, they would try to stomp out the selfish pervert in their midst.

"No!" she would scream, but a dozen arms would hold her. As she writhed, someone would jab a needle in her arm, and the circle of rage would dissolve.

A hand shoved June as if she were a cart, jolting her from her horror fantasy. She had reached the top, and before her spun a roulette wheel of glass compartments. She slipped into an opening that flicked past, and the door deposited her outside. As fast as she could, she walked away. If she sprinted, she might attract eyes.

On the broad sidewalk, the oppressive day was starting to show its weariness. The heat could still have drained most bodies, but the sun seemed to doubt it could burn much longer. Filthy men huddled under a railway bridge, waiting to welcome the dark. No one watched June as she rushed past, trying to put as many bodies as she could between her and that throbbing touch.

Beside her, discount stores with packed windows extended far back from the street. If someone were tracking her, these caves crammed with clothes might help her to disappear. She stepped into a shop whose window held a blouse like the one she wanted. Grown-up. Not shiny, not floppy, just dark and pleasingly close-fitting.

Neat and garishly lit, the store hummed with energy that spoke of a manager's close watch. Between symmetrically placed wheels of clothes, the white floor reflected fluorescent light. Handwritten signs said in thick, straight letters, "Return all unpurchased items to an attendant. We'll put them back where they go." Bulky women squeezed between racks as though caught between cogwheels in a factory.

June followed a gray lady in white whose rasping breaths marked the way to the blouses. Fingering the circle of hanging sleeves filled June with furtive pleasure. Most of the blouses shimmered in summer corals, some in cooler aquas and greens. From the sleeves' length, she knew they were tents, sewn for bodies two times her size. To find a small blouse, she flicked through systematically, freeing shirts that were shoved toward the center.

"May I help you?"

A warm tenor voice sounded behind her. A heavy young man was smiling as though pleased by her concentration. Over his round face, his brown hair curled damply. He couldn't have been more than twenty-five, maybe a student earning rent money.

"Oh, I'm looking for small blouses—black." Pulled from her thoughts, June fought to speak, as though knocked awake by an alarm.

"Try over here." The tall boy extended a thick arm ninety degrees past the spot where she was searching. "Try on as many as you want. Anything you don't take, just give back to me."

The manager loped off to help another woman, and June shifted her search to the place he had shown. In seconds, a small black blouse met her fingers—rippling silk with abalone buttons. The shimmer of those midnight-blue rounds woke blues and greens in the black. Above all, the scale of the blouse pleased her—the small collar, the short arms sloping to tight cuffs. Still, she groped on, determined not to miss others, and found the blouse's navy-blue sister. She also picked up a black cotton shirt with fine, waist-hugging darts.

June took the three blouses to a booth screened by a smudged canvas curtain. The makeup on the rough fabric looked fresh, and she pitied the manager, who, when he saw those smears, might feel as if someone had wiped her face on his shirt. As the silk slid against her skin, June's breathing slowed. The black blouse brought a sad elegance. Over the blue-black glow, her pale face shone defiantly.

The mirror reflected handwritten signs high behind her: "Like what you see? Then buy it. We call police."

Her heart thumped, and she reached for the blue blouse without bothering to read the rest. As she'd known, she didn't need to try on the navy-blue blouse or the crisp shirt with the tight darts. She had bonded with the abalone black. In a mental crane shot, she watched herself wearing it, scanning Didi's circle of mourners.

When she pulled the stiff curtain, she found the shop empty except for the disks of clothes. The other women had left, and the young manager had vanished.

"Hello?" she called, gripping the black blouse in her left hand and the rejects in her right.

The brown-haired boy must have been working in back, or maybe he'd gone to the bathroom. She would do him a favor and return the blouses. She took pride in her fail-free mental maps. On the jammed rack, she forced the hangers in so that they aligned perfectly with their neighbors. She waited at the register until the tall boy emerged, probably from a bathroom break. His eyes darkened as they focused on the black blouse hanging from her hand.

"How many shirts did you try on?" he asked.

"Three," she said. "I just want this one. I put the others back."

The heavy boy's breathing quickened. All friendship faded from his face.

"Did I or did I not tell you," he said, "to give me anything you didn't buy?"

How big he was. To see his eyes, June had to tilt her head all the way back.

"Did you not see the signs in the dressing room?"

His voice had risen to an ugly pitch. June's heart slammed her chest, but an inner switch dimmed the rest of her. Her voice emerged low, soft, calm.

"Yes," she said. "I'm sorry."

He shook his curly head in mock disbelief. He spread his feet slightly as though bracing to hit her as hard as he could.

"I didn't take anything," said June. "I wouldn't do that. Do you want to look in my pack?"

He towered over her, performing barely controlled rage. "Show me what you put back," he said disgustedly.

June led him to the rack and pointed to the neatly aligned navy and dart blouses.

"Open your pack," he ordered.

June hung the black blouse next to its friends so that she could free her hands.

"No!" he yelled. "Give that to me! What the fuck did I just say?"

June handed him the blouse, slipped the pack from her shoulders, and stooped before him to slide the zipper. He glanced inside.

"OK," he said. "You can go."

The black blouse shone against his fleshy arm. June closed her pack and rushed for the door. She dodged the bodies between her and the blue *U-Bahn* sign and slipped into the first train that rattled up.

"He's holding that beautiful blouse captive," June told Carolin the next day.

Under her acorn cap of brown hair, Carolin's green eyes glowed. "Are you going to rescue it?" she asked, her thin lips curving.

June never knew what Carolin thought of her adventures, which often brought battering. For someone too cheerful to be bright, Carolin caught the truth fast. Ever since that silk had slid over June's skin, the black-and-blue shimmer had become part of her body. When the soft sleeves had hung from the bully's hand, she had felt as though he had her daughter by the hair.

"I've got to go back there," she said. "He can't work every shift. Maybe if I just walk by ..."

Carolin's gaze shifted to the black leather couch, where her son Ingo's test kicks had quickened. The day-care center paid to watch her two-year-old had called at seven that morning to say they wouldn't open. The two teachers not on vacation had fallen ill, and everyone at Translate-OR had to take the consequence: a darting, shrieking, psychotic thing that made talk or thought impossible.

"Ingo, stop kicking!" called Carolin. "Where's your train?"

Ingo added his voice to the assault, emitting a sharp cry for each kick. June covered her ears. The piercing sound burned like a stab. She had never understood how anyone could learn to live with a child's voice.

"Ingo, stop! You're hurting people's ears!"

Carolin stooped to gather the wrecked train, which lay kinked like a broken snake. As she bent, her thick brown hair stayed stiff. She laid the train full-length along the small body, which stopped thrashing as Ingo tested the links between cars. June stayed crouched, her hands cupping her ears since the shrieks could start again any time. Near children who'd screamed or just-exploded fireworks, she shielded her ears, not knowing when the next arrow would pierce.

"It's OK." Carolin's warm hand touched her shoulder. "You don't have to be afraid of him. Did he hurt your ears that much?"

In the waiting room, the black leather tightened. The matching chairs drew closer together. On the taut table, light from the south window seared magazines kicked askew. Ingo hurt everything that was, but June had learned not to say so.

"You're trembling," said Carolin. "I'm sorry. He's angry. He doesn't like it here."

"Could you have stayed home with him?" asked June.

Carolin's hazel eyes lost their light. "I work the front desk. You can translate from home. I have to be here."

Ingo rolled off the couch and ran to Carolin with thudding steps. He seized her leg as an activist hugs a tree.

June straightened and slowly uncovered her ears. "Maybe someone else could work reception today," she said.

Carolin stiffened, and Ingo frowned up at her.

"Could you do my job?" she asked. "People think it's nothing. Dieter never even thought of taking him to work."

Ingo loosened his grip on Carolin's thigh and glanced between her and June.

"Have you asked him?" June said.

Carolin's tension fizzled to a laugh. "He runs a bank," she said. Her eyes warmed as she pictured Ingo in her husband's refined space.

Ingo ran to June, and an octopus seemed to wrap itself around her leg. As he smiled at her, she fought a panicked urge to kick herself free. Probably, the little brain behind that bright face couldn't imagine that anyone wouldn't love him. Like his mother's hair, Ingo's thick blond curls stayed stiff, damp peaks of set meringue. He shifted his grip, palpitating June's thigh. The tiny tentacles of this soft sea creature pleased her. Oh God. That handful of warmth. She tried to push Ingo back, but he clung fiercely.

"Come on, Ingo. June needs to work."

Carolin disengaged her son as though she knew of a hidden catch. June fled to her office, wishing Carolin had had a chance to say whether she should save the black blouse.

In the *Hof*, a woman in a flouncy purple skirt raised the lid of the yellow dumpster. She squinted at a red plastic cup and tossed it, and it landed with a faint crack. June was translating a divorce settlement for a Canadian scientist applying for dual citizenship. To prove she was detached, the physicist needed an official translation of her divorce papers, which opened a window to a hideous life. While driving their car sixty miles an hour, her husband had screamed, "Why can't you make a baby, you fucking bitch?" In English, June felt the words resound in that sealed space, but she couldn't hear them in German. Translation software conjured a dim ghost of the words: "*Warum kannst Du kein Baby bekommen, du verdammte Schlampe*?" (Why can't you receive a baby, you damned slut?). Her captor wasn't talking about receiving a gift or about being damned. In this man's mental world, his wife created a baby, and she fucked with a lusty dog's energy. In degrading her, the brutal man had given her a lot of agency.

Of course he had wanted her to have a baby, the way he probably wanted to break her feet. June had never understood why women had children—shrieking, annihilating fiends. Motherhood brought two decades of contempt, insults, accusations, and slave labor. Getting pregnant meant volunteering for a lobotomy, walking freely into a torture chamber. Giving birth was the ultimate idiocy, swapping identity and freedom for a hormonal mirage. The child, like the man, would take and despise. No one could be a good enough slave.

Funny, Carolin had thought June was scared of Ingo. That was what Margie had said back in Cleveland. On a frigid day, Tina brought her baby to the Writing Center, and people rushed to admire the new human. Teachers and students bent, awestruck, and June tried to see what inspired them. In the carriage, a writhing grub stirred a blue blanket, its pink mouth gaping in an effort to eat the world. When its blue eyes opened, they focused on June in the mosaic of faces above.

"Hey, he likes you!"

Margie jostled her. June stiffened, but in a clump of people, how did you tell your boss not to touch you? She'd been lucky to land this lectureship in writing after three years spent seeking German studies jobs. Her thesis on Thomas Mann's descriptions of sound had impressed no one—at least not enough to try her in a tenure-track job. Her adviser had urged her to retool, to learn the theory and technology of writing programs. June suspected he was glad to be rid of her, since her joblessness meant he'd failed too.

June couldn't eat and pay rent on what she earned, so she survived by translating and editing. She liked the online work better than her struggles with students, who saw her class as a mountain to be climbed on the way to money. With science books, she felt most at ease—no shrinking, no suggesting, no hedging. On pages that would fill heavy textbooks, she met earnest sentences saying, "This is what is."

This month, she was editing her favorite book so far, an introduction to the auditory system. The author, a female neuroscientist, described the cochlear hair cells so well that their soft fingers rippled through June's mind. Guided by words, June stroked the cells, sloped anemones whose tremors channeled life's wonders. People came into the world with thirty thousand hair cells, and they could make no more before they died. The liquid dance of these trees caught the sighs of wind in grass and the scratch of squirrels' claws grasping tree bark. Each day, these tendrils could be slashed by sound scythes. Firecrackers. Sirens. Burst balloons. High-pitched sounds could slice them like razors. Alarms. Electronic feedback. Worst of all, a child's screams.

Tina's baby opened and closed its mouth like a panicked fish on a pier. Its nose wrinkled, and its balled fists forced their way out from under blue fuzz. June tried to pull back, but the bodies behind her held her tightly in place. The baby's scream tore the air. June cried out and clapped her hands to her ears. All eyes shifted to her, reproachful and amused.

Margie shook her head, chuckling. "Come on, June. You don't have to be afraid of a baby. The guy I failed last term made more noise than that."

June crouched, rigid, as though someone had lashed her with a branch. The baby's voice tightened to cement-cutting violence. No living force could have pried June's hands from her ears. Glenda, her office mate, looped her arm through June's and pulled her back into the Writing Center.

"It's OK," said Glenda. "The baby's all right. Tina's got him now. He's fine."

Glenda stared at June, her brown eyes mustering strength that belied her limp hair. Experimentally, June softened her fingers. Sure enough, the shrieks had collapsed into sputters. She withdrew to their office, whose smell of books calmed her. Glenda turned her chair to face June, as though awaiting a confession.

"She needs a canister," said June. "A soundproof canister. Everyone with a baby should have one. It should be required by law. Dogs that bite have to wear plastic cones. Everyone with a baby should have to carry a canister, and if the thing screams, pop it in there till it's quiet."

"But the baby would suffocate," said Glenda. She rotated her chair left, then right.

"Not that fast," said June. "There could be a ventilation system. Or if not, oxygen deprivation would shut it up quick. It could come out as soon as it stopped screaming."

The flow of words brought exhilaration she hadn't felt in months.

"But the babies could be brain-damaged," said Glenda. "No one would agree to that."

Under her gray wool dress, her breathing quickened as though she were seeing the baby batteries in *The Matrix*.

"Then they shouldn't take their babies out in public," said June, "where they hurt people and disrupt everything. A scream that kills hair cells—that's assault. No different than slashing someone with a knife."

"Wait a minute." Glenda's voice deepened. "Are you saying women with babies should stay home—like prisoners—until their kids are how old? Ten?"

June raised her eyes to a Vermeer painting over Glenda's

desk, a watchful beauty with parted lips. "No, five maybe. It varies. Just till they know not to scream."

"And would you apply the same rule to men?" asked Glenda.

June shrugged. "Sure, whoever's in charge. Whatever it takes to stop public screaming."

Glenda smiled. "OK, if I get pregnant, I'll go online first thing and look for a soundproof box."

June's stomach tightened. "No, I'm not kidding. If you have a baby, you have to take the consequences. No one who cares about her work could have a baby."

Glenda turned her chair 180 degrees and reentered the essay on her screen.

Margie called June to her office a week later, a confrontation June had known was coming. Glenda's shadowed look had spread until not one colleague brightened when June approached. Glenda hadn't recorded their conversation, but in this realm of words, her mind had absorbed all. Why had June said, "No one who cares about *her* work could have a baby," if she thought men had the same obligation to stay home?

"I wanted to use an indefinite pronoun," said June, "which shouldn't have to be *his*."

"Then you should say *their*."

Margie's New York roots gave rise to a smoky vowel. June kept her eyes on Margie's set face. *Their* for an individual sounded crude. June's silence seemed to arouse Margie more than any reply might have done.

"Babies in canisters?" Color rose to her face. "Suffocating babies? Because they bother your ears? That's Nazi shit."

Red splotches spread over Margie's cheeks, with one tight focus under each eye. June stared, waiting to see what would happen.

"You expect the world to rearrange itself to suit your sensitive ears? Maybe *you* should carry the canister and creep into it when you can't stand the noise."

"I'm thinking of everyone." June's voice wavered. "I'm trying to stop everyone's pain."

The quiver in her voice seemed to calm Margie's fury.

"All babies cry," she said. "You did. No one likes it. But it's not a crime. It doesn't cause pain. *You* do, when you overreact."

"I have a right to defend myself," said June. "Screams damage my ears."

"Yeah, right," said Margie. She picked up a printed essay on her desk and dropped it with a plop.

Later that semester, June received a letter saying her contract wasn't being renewed. Her evaluation indicated she was uncollegial and showed signs of misogyny. With a lawyer, she might have fought the accusations, but the academic world had lost its appeal. The science publishers respected her editing, and on a German listserv, she found the Translate-OR job. In midwinter, she gladly left Cleveland's snows for Linberg's glittering ice. She loved her new job communing with words, and to keep it, she refrained from saying that babies should be sealed in plastic boxes.

Carolin must have performed some trick to lull Ingo into silence. His shrieks stopped jabbing, and June's heart slowed as she ceased to brace herself. She stayed alert, though, unsettled, and jumped when heels cracked across the Hof. Waiting for external noises, she couldn't hear the voices showing how English thoughts sounded in German. The German counterpart of the Canadian eluded her, a man who wanted his wife's lust geared toward reproduction. What would he say to smash her sense of self? June rolled a pen between her palms, since its ink conjured more voices than a computer.

When she left the office, she went to the Fine Arts Museum, which stayed open Thursdays until eight. In Linberg, she knew of no place more hushed. Most parents sensed their kids would hate its vast rooms, where you could only stare at mute pictures. If some poor fool brought in a screamer, the irate looks of guards drove the offenders out. The Fine Arts Museum drew few people under thirty, who made most of the world's noise. The modern art museums lured more encroaching bodies than the *U-Bahn,* but these echoing halls of gold angels begged you to fill their space with ballet. More than once, June had pirouetted when a guard wasn't looking. She favored rooms with the fewest eyes, unwatched, unentered by patrons. Sensing a body that could hit, stomp, scream flooded the space of her thinking.

In these bright halls that smelled of paint, the German galleries offered the tenderest silence. The self-assured folk in black hats sought no eyes to affirm their being. They tolerated June as a kindred spirit who felt happiest when unseen. Greeting the nobles, she circled in measured steps as though gliding through a courtly dance.

What would the angry man call his wife in German? Words floated toward her, but she couldn't recognize them until she could hear. She would have to compromise: the standard term *Schlampe* would show her competence, but the brutality of his words demanded more.

As she entered a room of medieval men, a watchful guard froze her thoughts. Unlike most, he stood erect and still with a seasoned soldier's posture. His slim body seemed made for his blue uniform, which hung like a fitted suit. Though he must rarely have seen daylight, his brownish skin warmed the dark eyes studying her. When their eyes met, he shifted his gaze toward a painting on the far wall. Without breaking rhythm, June continued her circle, syncing her paces with her breaths. No more words drifted up. Her mind could do nothing but sense the black eyes tracking her around the room.

"Have you noticed this picture?"

June started, even though she half expected the low voice. The guard was pointing toward the picture he'd glanced at: a tired old man in a black cloak. The man gripped a wooden panel as though he wanted to vault himself from the frame. With silver hair and glowing skin, he resembled the guard, but the thin man walking toward June couldn't have been more than thirty.

"This one?" asked June, pointing toward the imprisoned man.

"Yes." The guard's drawn face brightened. "Look at that fur—the way the hairs part in the draft."

"Yeah, the poor guy had to sit there so long," said June. "Looks like he wanted to get out."

"Think of the artistry!"

The guard's energy tightened. His stiff fingers approached the tan and white fur. June braced herself for an alarm's stab.

"Think how long it must have taken to paint hair like that."

No alarm shrieked. The impassioned guard must have known just how close he could come without making the fur scream for help.

"Yeah, it looks soft—fluffy. If I stroked it, it would feel like a cat."

"No!" His voice sharpened. "I mean how long it must have taken him to paint fur that you can feel and smell. Fur that moves when you breathe. Who takes time nowadays to learn anything that well?"

June stiffened. He was saying no to her thoughts. Even after he'd hijacked them, they still weren't good enough.

"A lot of people take time to learn things," she said. "Everyone gets to be good at something."

The guard's taut body loosened as though he'd sought gold and found pebbles. "I guess you're right," he said. "I'm sorry. I've seen you here before. I thought you like art."

"I do," said June, hating her formality. She hated his

invasion more. "I'm going to keep going now," she said. "Have a good night."

"You too."

The guard smiled. He was really quite young, unable to hide his sadness. His air of correctness made him seem older.

The next room held one of June's favorite paintings, an image of female transformation. On the left side, gray women were carried toward a pool—one in a wheelbarrow—where they splashed in a water ballet. When they climbed out, all pink and golden, they donned red robes and frisked with men in bushes. Their life-seeking movement made June laugh. The men in the painting wanted their women young, bad enough to schlep them to this fountain. None of the women objected as their hanging-gourd breasts tightened to globes. Sucking children had stretched their bodies until no one loved them as they were. Rejuvenated, the ladies wanted to dress, eat, fuck—in that order—which would start the cycle again. In a deep green bush, a woman in red smiled at her hungry partner.

The words came: *"Du fickende Schlampe, warum kannst Du mir kein Kind geben?"* (You fucking slut, why can't you give me a child?). That was the thought—to channel women's life force so that it flowed for men alone. To lust, to think, to bear children—all to celebrate men.

No one was going to direct June's movements. No one was going to steer her thoughts. Satisfied with her translation—for now—she began a letter: "To the director of the State Museums, German Ministry of Culture …"

June stretched and turned in a ballet pose. The Fountain room was unguarded.

Birgit squinted, worried by June's translation. Did she have to say, "*Du fickende Schlampe*"? It seemed redundant since, after all, fucking was what *Schlampen* did. June assured her she needed that extra word. A slap hurt differently than a punch, and the ex-husband's words had been thrown for maximum sting. Birgit conceded, letting June prevail in matters of an English word's feel. June left the office buoyant, ready to rescue the black blouse.

When she emerged from the *U-Bahn,* the tunnel was pulsing with dark tones. A Russian man was playing Bach's D-minor toccata on his accordion. Short and plump, with cropped brown hair, he pumped rhythmically, his eyes closed. With his nose raised, he moved his head from side to side, as if he could smell the tones.

June stopped dead, and a damp body struck her from behind.

"*Blöde Kuh!* Stupid cow!" snarled a male voice.

June hummed the dark D until it resonated in every cell. Somber melodies danced around it like shadowed leaves in gusty wind. The Russian's thick fingers sent the notes spiraling. June recognized the man, who usually chose his spots well. In corners where hard walls pressed together, his instrument became a cathedral organ. What had brought him to this stifling tunnel in one of the poorest parts of town? The hot air tossed his somber sounds listlessly. Bach's toccata needed the clean, cold air of late fall.

In college, a weird student in a black cape had played the D-minor toccata each Halloween. Dramatically, he had spread his arms like wings as he played the university organ. The pale student had called himself Dr. Death and worn his black cloak to each class. When he'd spun the toccata Halloween night, hundreds of students had chanted, "Death! Death! Death!"

An angry arm shoved June aside, so that her shoulder knocked the concrete wall. She couldn't move on her own, held in place by the brown chords from another world. From a sticky stain where the floor met the wall, the stench of urine crept upward. The Russian accordionist opened his blue eyes, which focused on hers. Didi's eyes—unanswerable blue questions. The musician nodded, and his face dissolved as June's eyes filled with tears. She drew a rough breath and, in the music's swirls, sought the guiding D. Scarcely breathing, she stayed rigid until the music settled on the dark tone.

June dug in her pack and dropped a euro in the man's case, which lay spread like a stiff butterfly.

"*Dobro*," she murmured. "*Spasivo*."

Her voice barely sounded, but the musician smiled.

June worried she might not find the right shop in this strip of deep, narrow stores. She recognized its blouses instantly, though—captives crowding their cell window. Until now, she had felt like an action hero saving a black-haired beauty from a brute. As she peered between sleeves in the front window, she tracked his heavy movements. No other bodies were dodging the clothes racks. She would have to face the beast alone. June snuffed up her tears and pushed through the shop door.

The manager turned to face her, and instantly, his face hardened. He looked younger, rounder than she'd remembered, and fear flashed beneath his calm. What did he think she was going to do? Inside her, a smile rose.

"What do you want?" he asked.

"I want to buy that black blouse. The one I tried on the other day." Her voice rang steady and clear.

"What black blouse?" His contempt smoldered.

"The blouse I tried on a few days ago—when I had to leave."

The curly-haired boy stood waiting for her discomfort to unnerve her.

"You can look," he said. "I don't know if you'll find it. We sold a lot of blouses this week. But you'll have to leave that pack with me."

June wished she could run. The black pack strapped to her body held her phone, her wallet, her diary, and her keys. Without it, she would have no more traction in the world than the bodies lolled on the sidewalk.

"I can't—everything I have is in this pack," she said.

June couldn't draw enough breath. The manager pointed

a thick arm to a sign over the register: "Leave your packs, large purses, and trolleys here. We'll watch them for you."

He spread his legs to take a broader stance. "You think rules just don't apply to you?" he asked. "You shop here, you obey store policy."

His belly rose and fell. June pulled off her pack and clutched it.

"What's wrong with you anyway?" He tapped his middle finger to his right temple. "You're like a kid in a grown-up body. I can't believe you came back here."

June held her pack as though he wanted to peel it from her breast.

"I want to buy that black blouse." Her voice was failing.

"OK, fine. Give me your pack."

He extended a determined arm. June pulled the pack from her body, and he grasped its exposed loop.

"Go ahead," he said. "I'll give this back when you're done."

June drifted toward the blouse's rack. The absence of her pack crushed her chest so that she could draw only small breaths. The manager's eyes burned like lasers, searing into her searching hands. He'd been right that in the past few days, he had given many blouses new homes. June recalled forms and colors as well as words, and few of the abalone black's cohort remained. To irk the manager, she slowed her rhythm. She mustn't miss her grackle-black friend. She would flip through each hanger of every rack until she held the blouse in her hand.

As she fingered the plastic hooks, she saw no black shimmer. She finished one circle and started another. No black, only coral and green. Blue black belonged to this heat even less than Bach's D-minor chords.

The manager lumbered off to the back, leaving her pack unattended. She must have looked too obsessed to steal. Willing herself to breathe, she picked up her pace.

In a rack far from the black blouse's home, she found its navy-blue sister. She paused as her eyes welled with tears. She felt as though she'd found the sibling of a friend murdered by Nazis. Didi had forbidden her to speak of the war. Didi had had his rules too. She couldn't ask him about the Third Reich, especially his family's role in it. She couldn't discuss his wife's behavior unless he raised the issue himself. She couldn't reflect on his past women, and he protested if she dissected past men. The best thing about Didi was that he wasn't always there. When he wasn't, her thoughts could roam freely.

June continued her search, clutching the plastic neck of the blue silk blouse she would take home. Even if she found her blue-black friend, she was going to save its cooler sister. Machinelike, she ground through the disks of clothes. The manager reemerged and watched, arms folded. She found the dart blouse but left it hanging. The stiff cotton would have turned her to a triangle.

As she scanned the last rack, she sensed that she and the manager had synced their breaths. No magpie wing flashed; no midnight blue shimmered. Some other small woman must have bought the black blouse, or maybe he had hidden it to spite her.

"Are you going to take that?" he asked flatly.

"Yeah," she answered.

From behind the counter, he retrieved her pack. She checked to see how much cash she had.

"It's all there," he said disgustedly.

She paid him fifty euros, which she had withdrawn to fuel her for the whole next week. If she had used her credit card, he would have known her name. He mustn't know her. That was her rule.

Saturday morning, the heat pressed so close that June could barely breathe. The navy-blue silk clung to her skin, twisted by a black skirt that turned as she walked. By noon, the temperature would reach 100 degrees, stunning Linberg's persistent life. The day felt too hot for death, but the gray and black crows in the trees looked as though they might drop any moment.

June followed black figures moving measuredly toward a walled cemetery. Didi's family had arranged a traditional funeral in one of Linberg's hidden graveyards. The ant trail of mourners passed through grilled gates in a sandstone wall eight feet high. In this forest of graves, the dark stones stood so well concealed she could have passed without knowing they existed.

Several hundred people pushed into the chapel, where a nephew flashed pictures from Didi's life. June recognized the blue eyes on his two-year-old face, whose playfulness already had a cutting edge. In seconds, the mischievous baby morphed into a man, since the slide master sensed the force of the heat. Drops of sweat slid down the back of June's thighs. Bodies pressed her from every side, radiating warmth like black coals.

Even surrounded by mourners, she spotted Didi's wife, clutched by her protecting family. Tall and strong, she stared in shock at pictures of herself smiling at Didi. Each new picture brought a burst of sobs, a gut-driven animal howl. Her mother and brother held her as though she might blow apart from her grief. In wet waves, murmurs of sympathy rose with each fresh image. Didi at his computer, glancing up mockingly. Didi singing, his mouth open wide. Didi deep in the woods, his eyes shut to maximize his pleasure in black bread and cheese.

Escape from the chapel brought no relief, since the heat had intensified. June sucked in air that felt inert, unable to support life. Thirsty yellow jackets wove Vs in the air, approaching mourners' salty, wet skin. June joined a line creeping silently toward Didi's grave. As people reached the hole, each one took a red rose in one hand and a fist of dirt in the other and dropped both onto the polished coffin. A faint rhythm rose as sand and leaves whispered against varnished wood.

In a nearby lot, a worker was dismantling a wall brick by brick. Between the knocks of his hammer, cheerful twangs rose from a radio that kept him moving. Down the street, a yellow crane extended its stiff arm toward a scaffolded building site. Like a dragonfly perched on end, it offered sheetrock to workers with outstretched hands. From the distant site, the heavy air brought a thud, a cry, a faint clank.

June peeled the blue blouse from her chest and flapped it to fan herself. Only ten more bodies stood between her and the deep, square pit. She had hoped she might learn something about Didi, who had controlled access to his life. In the set faces, she recognized singers whose pictures he had shown her. Even in the stifling chapel, their songs had bloomed like dahlias. Some of the grim men must have been Didi's colleagues, of whom he'd told dark stories. Since no one dared speak, each one kept his secrets. If they were thinking of Didi, their dim eyes hid their thoughts.

As June approached the grave, the rhythm of soft thuds gained force despite its dragging pace. The line moved slowly because after dropping dirt, each mourner had to speak with Didi's family. They had announced his funeral on Instagram, on X, trying to summon everyone he had ever known. Maybe they had sensed his hidden currents and, seeing their last chance, wanted to scan the crowd.

Feeling as though she were being filmed, June stooped and grasped a wilted rose. With her right hand, she scooped up warm sand, which brought more pleasure than the barbed stem. She tossed the dirt and the flower together, so that they struck the gleaming chestnut with one soft sound. She wiped her right hand on her leg, where it left a brown smear.

Drawing a deep breath, she stepped toward Didi's wife, who stood flanked by supporting relatives. Despite her crumpled face, she stood upright. Her moss-green eyes glowed with strange light.

"I'm sorry." June exploded in tears.

Didi's wife placed a warm hand on June's shoulder.

"You poor thing," said the wife's mother, whose green eyes pierced deep.

"How did you know him?" asked Didi's wife.

"I translated some work for him. We translated together." June's voice wobbled.

"His translator! Even his translator came!" Didi's wife pressed June in a hug as tight as the first one he had given her.

"Yes," murmured his wife's mother. "That's the kind of person he was."

The wife released her, and June looked into eyes lit by unaccountable joy.

"Please stay in touch with us. His choir created an account—Friends of Didi—so we can stay connected."

"Sure," said June. "I'll watch the page. I'm sorry."

She waved off a yellow jacket wiggling on the wife's arm. Remembering the people trapped behind her, June stepped aside.

Beyond the wall, the yellow crane clanked, and the worker's hammer broke a brick. June looked up and noticed a dark, lean woman scanning her. The intent woman had sung with the choir, and her body hummed with fierce energy. A few paces off, she must have heard every word of June's exchange with Didi's wife. The woman squinted as though recording June's image and nodded to herself. She turned away toward a young blonde singer, laying long fingers across the woman's arm.

June closed her eyes and sucked in a searing breath. Behind her, the soft patter continued as sand and flowers buried bright wood.

No stern policeman came to rap on June's door. A week slipped by and then another. She had been expecting a tall female officer with hair pulled back in a tight ponytail. The avenging statue would want to know why she had enjoyed a handful of warm flesh. Flesh that belonged to a thirteen-year-old body. Flesh she shouldn't imagine, let alone grasp. That museum guard she'd accused had more disciplined hands than her pleasure-seeking paws. And why had she tried to steal two shirts from a businessman struggling in a rough district? Why had she come to Linberg to act like a Viking, when she could grope and steal in her own land? Germany was revoking her residency.

"No!" she gasped.

The powerful policewoman grasped her neck and shook her, strangling her scream. June spiraled through horror fantasies that left her panting, but the policewoman never came.

For weeks, June avoided Circle Center as though its air glistened with COVID drops. She shunned the gaping avenue that housed the brown-haired bully's shop. Instead of going to the Fine Arts Museum, she visited smooth, staring Egyptian sculptures. For minutes, she circled Nefertiti, whose lean self-assurance reminded her of the dark woman at Didi's funeral.

On Facebook, Friends of Didi bloomed with memories in every color. Then, slowly, the posts became less frequent.

"I wish I could send him pepper-and-mushroom pizza in the afterlife," wrote June.

One viewer responded, "Does Uber Eats deliver there?"

Soon after that, the garden withered.

June chewed her way through technical translations, which Birgit was now assigning her. As she sought words, she felt herself pulled toward the rings of Circle Center. The basement food court had always been one of her favorite spots to write. So far, no one had noticed her sin, maybe not even the girl herself. After a week, most security cameras recorded new images over their old footage. If she returned and wasn't seized, maybe the horror fantasies spinning through her head would stop.

On a ninety-degree September day, she decided to take the risk. She climbed out of the *U-Bahn* one stop early so she could peer into the angry boy's shop. Despite the draining heat, his window now displayed black and brown plaid jackets for fall. Between the legs of black pants, she glimpsed him contemplating one of his commanding signs.

June's bladder burned, and she hurried into Circle Center, whose down escalator was, mercifully, clear. When she left the bathroom, she felt too restless to write. Maybe she could explore the rings of stores first. At the foot of the up escalator, a crowd was pooling, since its sliding steps had suddenly stopped. June joined a group edging their way into a line creeping upward.

"The elevator's out too," said an old woman in a tremulous voice.

The arms emerging from her coral blouse were as thin and dry as her fragile legs. In oversized white sneakers, she looked as though she had fled a home by slipping on the first shoes she saw. June found herself shoved into line behind her, breathing the rancid smell of her greasy hair. Slowly, the woman raised her right foot to the first step, which had frozen just above floor level. With spotted hands, she clutched the black rails until her more timid left foot found the second step. The man climbing ahead of her had reached the middle, and murmurs rose behind June's back.

"She ought to be in a wheelchair."

"If she were, she'd be here all night, with no elevator."

"With no elevator, she wouldn't be *down* here."

An insistent body pressed June's back. Instinctively, she tapped the woman's curved shoulder. The thin body started. June raised her arms to catch her, but the stooped woman held fast to the rails.

"May I help you?" asked June.

She peeled bony fingers from the left rail and slipped onto the step beside her. A heavy man climbed into the space that June had just vacated. She and the tense woman now formed a plug, blocking everyone's way up. If June had stayed put, people might have squeezed by. That would have left the woman like a branch in a stream, a thing that blocked force until it snapped.

Clenching her teeth, the old woman raised a trembling foot that stopped just short of silver grooves. June wrapped one arm around a waist that held almost no flesh. The man's hot belly pushed June's back.

"Try again," she muttered.

The white sneaker met the metal edge but paused, unable to slide forward. June released the woman's waist and slipped her hand under her trembling thigh. With the fat man so close behind her, the failing woman couldn't fall back. June heaved, and the hapless foot settled onto the striped step.

"I'm so ashamed," murmured the woman, shaking.

"Come on," growled the man below.

June turned and looked into his flushed face. "Please, can you help us?" she asked. "Please don't let us fall back."

She wrapped her arm around the brittle body and heaved, and the white sneaker met its partner on the silver step.

June remembered an image from a watching camera at one of Linberg's worst *U-Bahn* stops. Late at night, a boy had kicked a woman downstairs by slamming his foot into her back. News stations played the clip over and over—the dark leg seeking its target, the limp body in flight. As June watched, she could feel the blow to her back, the breathless fall, the cement smash. It turned out the boy hadn't known the woman, who would never again move with ease. Maybe he'd wanted to see how far she could fly; maybe he didn't think women should walk around freely.

June gripped the old woman's waist. Her fetid smell made June's stomach heave.

"Was there a time when you wanted to walk upstairs?" June asked. "Something good up top?"

Thin ribs shuddered under June's hand. She had stirred a laugh.

"When Hermann was sick," said the woman. "I used to bring him food. He was so glad to see me."

June didn't ask whether Hermann was a scared boy or a felled husband. Either way, he had probably craved the food more than the provider.

"Hermann's up there," said June. "He's waiting. Hermann wants to see you."

The old woman raised a leg. The white sneaker tapped silver grooves. Several steps down, a baby shrieked. With a sharp pull, June heaved the tense body to the next step.

"What did you make him?" she whispered.

The old woman smiled. "Stuffed peppers. He liked those."

A man then. A boy would have winged them at the wall to watch the compressed rice explode.

"Fuck this!" A tall, angry girl pushed past.

A backpack slammed June's face. She cried out, and a bony hand grasped her arm.

"Are you all right, dear?"

Eight steps to go. The fat man behind raised his arms to help with each upward shove. The cloth covering the weak thighs grew wet as the old woman shook with sobs.

"Almost there," said June.

The trembling woman raised her eyes. In a burst of strength, she climbed the last steps almost alone. June couldn't tell how much she and the pushing man helped. They had merged into one climbing thing.

With a tired arm, June pulled the woman aside, and a stream of bodies surged upward. Protectively, she grasped the crying body, whose shaking slowly ceased. In the crowd flowing toward the circling doors, the baby's cry turned keen. June clapped her hands to her ears. Liberated, the old woman shuffled toward the whirling glass that would set her free.

ACKNOWLEDGMENTS

I am grateful to the friends who gave generously of their time to read the stories of *D Minor*. First, I would like to thank my former adviser from the Warren Wilson MFA Program, David Haynes, whose recommendations have always been transformative. I owe a debt to my Warren Wilson buddy, Terri Leker, who has done so much to encourage me as a writer. I thank Rita Charon, who took time from her work on narrative medicine to tell me what a cat's teeth can do to a human hand. Any errors I have made in applying her medical knowledge are mine alone. I have benefited from neuroscientist Nina Kraus's inspiring descriptions of the auditory system in her book, *Of Sound Mind*, and from the thoughts of biologist Scott Gilbert and cognitive literary scholar Lisa Zunshine. I am grateful to my former student, poet Richie Hofmann, for his comments on the opening poem, and to composer Shawn Kirchner for his reflections on the key of D minor. Finally, I offer my greatest thanks to my father, Arthur Nye Otis, Jr., and to his mother, organist and pianist Ella Willaume Otis, who bequeathed to me their sense of hearing.

Printed in the United States
by Baker & Taylor Publisher Services